red girl rat boy

Also by Cynthia Flood

The Animals in Their Elements
My Father Took a Cake to France
Making a Stone of the Heart
The English Stories

red girl
rat boy

stories
Cynthia Flood

A JOHN METCALF BOOK
BIBLIOASIS
Windsor, Ontario

FIRST EDITION

Library and Archives Canada Cataloguing in Publication

Flood, Cynthia, 1940-
     Red girl rat boy / Cynthia Flood.

Issued also in electronic format.
ISBN 978-1-927428-41-2

     I. Title.

PS8561.L64R43 2013   C813'.54   C2013-901996-0

 Canada Council   Conseil des Arts
for the Arts   du Canada

 Canadian   Patrimoine
Heritage   canadien

 ONTARIO ARTS COUNCIL
CONSEIL DES ARTS DE L'ONTARIO
50 YEARS OF ONTARIO GOVERNMENT SUPPORT OF THE ARTS
50 ANS DE SOUTIEN DU GOUVERNEMENT DE L'ONTARIO AUX ARTS

Biblioasis acknowledges the ongoing financial support of the Government of Canada through the Canada Council for the Arts, Canadian Heritage, the Canada Book Fund; and the Government of Ontario through the Ontario Arts Council.

Edited by John Metcalf
Copy-edited by Allana Amlin
Typeset and designed by Kate Hargreaves

PRINTED AND BOUND IN CANADA

MIX
Paper from
responsible sources
FSC
www.fsc.org   FSC® C107923

To the memory of Jane Creighton
poet, writer, graphic artist
1956–2012

contents

To Be Queen

SIBLINGS KNOW THE SMELL OF EACH OTHER'S POO. We know who's ashamed of pimples or bum, scared of crane-flies and the dog two doors down. Thunder, too. The others overhear us scolded and ordered about, as we hear them. Who steals? Hates fatty meat? Lies to teachers? Has to take the garbage out every day for a week? Can't use the car? We know, and know our parents' look after quarrelling, their bedroom sounds. We know our sister Annie died. Blindfold, in a breath we'd all three recognize the air of our house, its smell on our return from summer vacation at the lake.

Bright familiar colours splashed on separate darknesses—I tried to explain to Ivan, an only child, how we were.

MY BIG SISTER WANTED RED FLOWERS, I wanted a Smartie cookie, and to give orders. Two wants to one, yet my advantage: Mum would surely give me a cookie later, be my slave, but Coral needed those reds now and Mrs. in that garden scared her. Grumbling, she agreed. I knew she would.

Up she went where I dared not, that highest kitchen shelf.

Ohhh full mouth! Crackling soft chocolate, brown-sugary peany burr.

Lots. Never enough. Gone.

"*Now,* Kenny!"

Out the back without brother Will seeing. Under a fence and over another (not allowed), oh oh suck poor pricked thumby, pick a flower for each finger and count to be sure. Mrs. coming! Through the hedge, along the alley (forbidden, cars), round to the front gate and Coral. She'd filled my worm-jar with water.

"Who said you could?" I didn't care really, let her go to the dumb birthday party.

Back inside, the house cool in summer.

Will sat on the couch holding a knife and a manual, wood-shavings littered about (not allowed, only in the basement). Spotty-face. Older, nearly another parent. To a small child, the family's a given, absolute, its spacing unremarkable: sixteen, (twelve), eight, four.

"Kenny, where've you been? You're filthy."

To the hot yard again, the tree house.

Did I see Coral come crying home?

The interrogation I did hear. *Why did you steal those roses for that girl? Why?* My sister wouldn't make herself more trouble by telling on me; I went on playing, and later got a cookie. Mum was too tired to be slave, though. Coral knew she had to, for a few minutes at least, but she wasn't good at it. Our mother spoke so convincingly.

"O magnificent prince, what is thy wish?"

Not another peany burr cookie, no point asking, teeth already brushed. Mostly, another storybook. Or Hangman, I Spy, Going on a Trip.

Once in a long while, "Tell about Annie?"

Mum's wording hardly altered. "Annie got sick, and she died just before her first birthday. Time for sleep, Kenny."

A gap, then.

Crossing the school playground with my babysitter (why? I'm not even in kindergarten), I meet Coral trailing a group of girls.

What a cute little boy! Isn't he just? My sister's look unreadable. It clears. "Kenny, do a somersault!" A recent learning, this. I love performance. *Look at him go!* Another roll. Applause. Coral wavers, pleased the girls are pleased, envious of me.

Can he go backwards? My attempt lands me flat on my back, giggling with sky above. *Tickle him!* They're on me. First I laugh, then there are too many eyes and fingers, open mouths, teeth. My few clothes loosen. I struggle. An older boy appears, high on his bike against the blue. His glance, contemptuous of little kids. He wheels off. I lie still, and the attack ceases.

Thus I learned that if you don't give a shit, or credibly pretend not to, even in defeat you have power. Ivan never believed that a child so young could know that.

Coral always cared too much, still does. Like Mum and Dad, she's got three kids plus one missing. Ads and agencies haven't worked. "Yet," she says firmly. Coral's siblings haven't added to the population, for reasons closely related yet not the same.

I remember. That new babysitter, *the bad woman* who made Mum get a job, had taken me for ice cream to soften me up. The playground was a shortcut home. I knew Mum judged its high slide dangerous, so I tattled, but she didn't stop working.

Another gap.

Each sibling privately recalls the first sight of Mum crying.

Her shoulders heaved in that awful hurting way, like when Will and I were playing tag and laughing and I fell, ripping open my knee.

"I believed they were nice girls!"

I ran far off, to the tree house. An old tarp made its roof, and I pulled that down around me to hide everything in the world except the ragged faded plastic. After an enormous time I re-entered the house.

Dad was just home from the mill. "Coral did what, Lorna?"

"Cut herself. I had to take her for stitches. Raymond, our ten-year-old daughter carved her foot with a paring knife."

Who? Dad was Ray.

"Why?" His lunch bucket landed on the kitchen counter. Ray and Lorna, king and queen, couldn't sound like this. Not allowed.

"To be queen for a day." A noise, not laughter. "In a clique."

"What?" Impatience rising.

More noise. "Blind, blind. Just like before."

"Lorna-a-a-a." My father put his arms around her. She shook him off.

Years later, Coral told me that she and Mum drove to Victoria the following weekend. They stayed in a bed and breakfast, had tea at the Empress, toured SeaWorld.

"Mum was so gentle! She kept saying, *You deserve a treat*, but all the time I felt those girls talking about me. I'd have to face them, at school."

Our parents were in their mid-twenties at my brother's birth, nearing forty at mine. Different people. For eight years Will and Mum and Dad lived elsewhere, the site of Annie's arrival and death. I've only seen photos of that home. She's not in any.

When Coral came, everyone moved to the house I knew, which Will left before I turned ten. My small childhood's big event: Mum's return to work. For him, what was big?

Like our mother I sleep poorly, walk and talk while enduring wakefulness. During my childhood she'd putter in the night kitchen, musing aloud about our health and school marks, her in-laws, next day's dinner, laughing sometimes.

Angry hissing sounded if Coral came in, late and rude. Dad never woke. Too tired.

The one time Will's voice rose right up the stairs— this was after the cutting, before *Carrie*—he wouldn't hush for Mum.

"*Take some responsibility?* Haven't you blamed me enough?"

Murmuring.

"You do too, Mum!" More quietly, "I wasn't there when Coral cut herself, either. She did that."

Our brother Will was long gone to the east coast, as far away as possible without actually exiting the country, on an autumn evening when Mum and Dad went out to play cards with friends.

Negotiations with my sister stalled, because she offered money only for the horror movie our parents wouldn't let me see. None for popcorn.

"Okay, I'll stick around so you and him can't slobber, yuck." Fun, yes, but really I didn't care what she and her boyfriend did.

"No you won't, Kenny!"

"Want me to tell Mum?"

She counted out the cash. I knew she would.

Carrie scared the bejeezus out of me, at age eleven. Bad nights followed. I overheard Mum ask Coral if she knew why, and my sister's negative answer. (*Carrie* also scared Ivan, a shared experience discovered soon after our meeting. We rented the movie, felt safe as we watched together.)

In late winter my sister went to visit Aunt Marlene at the lake and stayed for months.

"How come she's allowed to miss so much school?"

"No point getting angry," Dad answered. "Talk to your mother."

Who said only, each time, "Coral will be home soon, Kenny," and went on basting her perfect chicken or ironing her restaurant uniform. Her voice roiled my insides. So—frail? Not allowed. To change things, I tried the Annie-question.

Mum looked up, surprised. "She just got sick, Kenny. You know that. Annie didn't quite get to be one year old."

For the first time, I pushed. "But what did she die *of*?"

"Meningitis." Back to the chuckling fat in the roaster.

The word stopped me. How to spell it, past *m-e-n*? (Ivan thought my reaction strange, dearly strange.) Nor did I present another long-hoarded query, *Why isn't Annie in the albums*? Mum was queen, her intention to keep silence palpably stronger than my curiosity. Finding the word didn't bring the usual dictionary-satisfaction, either. In the decades since, I've read about the disease. It's tricky, wears masks. One symptom is cold hands.

That summer, Will made a visit home. With our parents we went to the lake for a family vacation, as usual, and to retrieve Coral, unusual. She and Will spent hours together. Much later, learning the word *solicitous*, I recognized how our brother had been with her.

When he flew back to Nova Scotia I went with him, for a visit. What did this cost our parents? I loved the flight.

Will was already building his house, by the shore. I helped. His workshop and its sweet smell of wood fascinated me. Amazingly, his hands and the buzzing machines formed bowls, plates, lamps, tables.

We talked of childhood. Trying to sound grown-up, I told how hard I'd taken Mum's return to work.

He laughed, not meanly. "For me, the biggest thing was the strike at the mill. Just like the song! *First we walked out, then we were locked out, then by a foul we were all but knocked out.*"

"Tell more!"

"Giving orders, are you? It lasted months. Dad got even more quiet. Meals got skimpy. Kenny, do you hear Mum talk in the kitchen at night?"

We moved on to that.

Another long gap.

When I was in high school Coral told how she'd once named a doll Annie. "I made her die, Kenny. Mum found me in the side-yard, burying."

"She got mad?"

A shrug. "Went into the house."

"Do you know what happened?"

"Just the doctor said it was too late."

We resumed Monopoly. Such gleeful laughter. For years Coral beat me, I beat her at checkers, at Scrabble we were well-matched. She didn't enjoy chess, my favourite. "It's like war." Exactly. In my later teens, Mum appeared the powerful queen and Dad the king, his moves so limited.

After Coral too left home, for an unapproved marriage, the concerns of Mum's insomniac monologues deepened. Or I understood them better. (*Fucking menopause!* shocked me, though.) *Why don't Will and his girlfriend live together? Poor Coral, with that man. What's wrong with Kenny?* The queen was free to speak more loudly, too. The prince had won a scholarship to university, while the king still slept heavily and had grown nearly deaf.

During law school, on one of my visits home she swore at length about Dad's heart, his doctors.

For once I knew what the big kids didn't. I told Coral, phoned Will.

At the funeral, he and I got past the awkwardness of brothers not often present to each other. Oh, I'd flown east, he'd flown west, but twelve years is a long way. Will was forty; I'd just passed my bar exams.

We cried for our father.

"And hasn't Mum got small, Kenny? Old."

I agreed, though in fact our queen was just getting started on those two projects. For some time we didn't notice her aging, preoccupied as we were with surveying the enormous blank in our lives shaped by our dead father. My need for Dad shocked me. (When Ivan to his surprise found that I was inessential, even in my rage I understood, knowing how ignorant one can be. What a pair.)

Soon after that death, Coral's guy dumped her at last. Her kids were teenagers, she their queen.

My brother and I found we'd both wanted to say *You're all better off without that loser,* but neither of us did, knowing our mother would issue that judgment. With Coral's children, I played all our old childhood games.

By then I'd started in labour law. Union work began to take me across the country; Will and I connected. His small house, long since finished, of course, looked beautiful. His partner—younger than he, definitely not a loser—lived with her kids in the nearby town. Earlier, I hadn't wondered about Will's choosing such an isolated site, didn't ask other questions either.

Now I did, still feeling privileged to watch him use the drill-press, the lathe.

"Why stay here? Partly this, Kenny." He waved towards the shavings on the floor, his wall of tools, the soft sheen of bowls. "And Jeanie's here. Dad didn't approve," another wave at all the wood, "of course. He always said—"

In unison, "*You've got to think about a pension!*" The king hadn't lived to collect his. We smiled a bit.

Looking back at Will's workspace as he was locking up, I said, "How Jeanie's kids must love this!"

"Children aren't allowed in here. Dangerous."

Twenty years after Dad died I slept in my childhood home one more time, just before we moved the queen off the board into care.

In the night I heard Mum, alone in their bedroom.

"Ray, I never understood, never. Her hands were cold. Will gone. The cutting, the other. And why's Kenny that way?" Sobs.

Coral wasn't in our house to hear her. Will wasn't either. Nothing for it: the youngest must get out of bed and cross the dark hall, must be slave.

Mum had forgotten I was home.

"Not sleeping, Kenny? Do you want some hot milk?" The old face red from crying. Arm in arm—she stepped with difficulty—we got slowly down to the kitchen. Ivan had taught me to sprinkle cinnamon. She enjoyed that.

At night now, there's no one to hear me talk. *And whose fault is that?* As Mum would say. She liked Ivan, as much as she could. They played aggressive Scrabble, laughing, sometimes even when I was out of town.

Ivan. Five years.

We met at the only orgy I ever attended. Another playground, bodies all over, the scents of flesh, excitement's edge crinkling with nerves, a man gazing down at me. Ivan's dreamy look: at once addictive. Probably I'd be in charge? The youngest, the pawn, always seeks control.

I was important to Ivan, yes, very, but, as it turned out, not necessary. At a disadvantage because I wanted him more than he wanted me, I figured fatherhood would subtract from the sum of us.

Ivan rejected my calculations. "I love you! I'm as surprised as you that I want a child so much." He looked about our living room, at the full wineglasses, as if they were novelties.

"Making your list for a fair division of the household goods?"

"Oh, Kenny. . ."

"Oh, Ivan, who suddenly wants so bad to be a daddy."

He grabbed my hand. "Can't you reach to this? For me? For once not be the star of the high school debate team?"

Briefly I failed to fake indifference. Ivan attempted comfort, but at the end said, "You're a loner, Kenny. You'll be fine."

The next time Will and I met, in his workshop with the maples outside and the Atlantic beyond, he swept the floor and set tools in order while I told about Ivan.

That done, I felt old enough to ask about Annie.

The broom stopped. "I was five. Dad was on strike, hardly ever home. I had a bad flu but was getting better fast. So, when Annie ran a high fever. . ."

"Mum assumed flu?"

Swish swish, the bristles. "If I hadn't been so healthy, she'd have worried more. Fact, Kenny. But I refused to live with guilt. Or to live anywhere near hers."

I held the dustpan. A small service for him.

Once in care, Mum went downhill fast.

Coral and I had planned to rent the house short-term. Then with tenants' eyes we inspected the small rooms. *No,* said the stained and collapsing furniture, the faded paint, the ancient water heater and the fridge that dripped. We began to clear the place for sale, talking and talking as we worked.

Once I reminisced about my somersaults in the playground, done for her, but Coral didn't remember that. Just then we were tackling the living room shelves, where, among much other detritus, the photo albums lived.

"Coral, you'll take these?"

Already she was paging through one volume.

"Look, Kenny! My eighth birthday! You were four."

Her Polaroid cake had turned orange, her dress cerise, and time had paled our official school pictures. How old-fashioned our family looked, by the backyard barbecue and at the lake—Will's big glasses, Dad's too, everyone's weird clothes and shoes. In every scene we were laughing.

An envelope fell out. Two tiny black-and-whites with rippled edges. High contrast.

"Who's she?"

"Silly! Mum, with weird long hair. Are those flowers on her head?" She frowned at the baby's face, shaded by a bonnet. Turned over the shiny squares. No names.

"Kenny. It has to be her."

We stared.

Coral dropped the photos as if they were alight. "Damn Annie, why the hell didn't she live? I wasn't enough, they needed her, and I made so much trouble!"

Crying, she let my arm stay round her.

"Take her to Will," wiping her eyes, "when you go next."

I had enlargements made for all three of us.

Flying no longer excites me. In the plane's washroom, the blurry mirror shows neither youthful charm nor aged dignity. Just a suit, a briefcase, a phone. Union delegates sneer, yet approve their lawyer's looks. Sometimes there's applause.

Will's workshop smelled good, as always.

I handed Annie over.

His turn to stare.

"Mum, so young? How I loved her long hair! See her daisy crown? I made that for her." He peered. "Wait now." At the window, he held the image to the light. "He's here." Relief, warmth, satisfaction.

Behind our mother and Annie, slightly to one side, almost blended into a shiny black hedge stood our father, stiff even then, his body ground down by the mill, smiling gently.

"Dad let me use his camera." Will's voice thickened. "That casing's the kitchen window of our house. Mum got Annie's new bonnet that day."

Excluded from this nostalgia, not even born, I waited in darkness for my brother to step down the years to me.

Eggs and Bones

THE EGGS HIT THE PAN. TOO MUCH SIZZLE. Probably he'd set the heat at 5 again, not 3. For sure he hadn't whisked the eggs long enough, she'd counted the strokes. He'd see too late that the mixture was streaky, then stir and disturb the setting process.

Kyra lay in their king-sized bed, listening to Norman cook.

Likely he's using butter *and* oil. Stupid. That metal spatula, skr-skr-skr. It'll wake Maeve. I can't bear it, truly. Why won't she sleep through the night? Oh lucky me with my mat leave! A whole year to enjoy my baby. Her birthday next week. Use the *plastic* one. Right there, in the utensil jar. That pan's scarred already.

The colic's over months ago but still she wakes, wakes, wakes. She has daytime naps, I'm exhausted, I sleep too. No work. I'm thirty. It's time.

He shouldn't scrape yet anyway. Just tip, slide the liquid under, but those eggs'll be nearly cooked now. Frizzled, more like.

For Norman, earplugs work, but even if I shove them in till I think they're touching my brain and move her crib right to the end of the hall I still hear Maeve. She's not hungry. Won't feed. Cries a while, sleeps again. I don't. I can't. The clock radio's turned to hide time rushing on, but in May the birds start at four. If I do sleep it's like an instant till she cries again.

What's he taking out of the fridge? Please not chorizo.

Not just my ears but all of me senses Maeve. Three floors away I'd feel her crying. Mushrooms? I'm starting to work from home. So many women want to do just that, so lucky me. Cheese? The office. I've tried to stay connected, but visiting there with Maeve feels unreal. Maybe once I get into my projects? How can I? In all the hours, where's the time? I need sleep.

Oh God he's slicing onion.

I will not rage about Norman's damned tibula, fibia, whatever. Not not not. Recrimination does no good, Kyra, especially to you. We all make mistakes, I've told you that easily five hundred times since it happened and he's been here, here in this small apartment 24/7 except for physio.

Raw cold onion wrapped in leather: my breakfast, after another hellish night.

Now Norman can get about, he takes Maeve out a bit so I can work. They just go to Starbucks. That's fine. I don't care. She crawls about and people say, "So cute!" I sleep, after setting the alarm so I can pretend to have been busy, but soon he'll go back to work. I can't bear it.

We need to get out of this. The weather's warmer these days.

The pan's in the sink, tap's running. Where the hell is my food?

Coffee's on. That's something.

I know, he's trying to wash off the mushy egg-scum. Won't work. The problem's deeper. He's overheated the pan, and that makes the fat form a hard scale all round, just where the sides curve up. It seems only a slight discolouration, but run a finger over the metal and it's rough, scabby.

Where? A park. The beach. Maeve loves sun. Sweet, her little dresses.

Further use causes more harm. Foods catch, stick on that scaliness, scorch. With uneven heat, the pan becomes unusable. Has to be tossed.

We'd take the bus. He won't like that. Maeve will love it.

Sluicing, sluicing. He's trying the scrubber. Now the dish-brush. Plastic in this situation isn't effective. How many times have I shown him?

I'm so hungry. So tired.

Ah. He's remembered baking soda. Dampen a soft cloth, dip it, rub.

Rub rub rub, soft, almost soothing, but how long? When will this end? Where's my food? Maeve'll walk soon. I can't bear it.

Now rinsing. Now stopped. Still no coffee. Somewhere beautiful. I want a new summer dress.

Beside her in the bed, the flung-back duvet created negative space around the shape of Norman. Maeve's father. Impossible.

Enough!

Kitchen smells juiced up Kyra's mouth.

From their bed to the stove was fifteen steps, but she got there in ten.

Leaning against the sink, Norman niggled at the pan, his gaze concentrated as when reading student papers.

On a white plate, a thick yellow envelope had split to ooze chorizo, onion, salsa, melted cheddar. Grabbing a fork and the food, Kyra shoved in one huge bite of red orange yellow before crying out. For the first time in their shared life, Norman had heated a plate. It slid from her hand to the counter's edge, stayed. Just.

For comfort, Kyra crossed her smarting fingers over her body and into her armpit while she glared and ate.

"Let's all go out," she said through a mouthful of eggs. Maeve cried.

HIS WIFE HAD PURCHASED FOR THE OCCASION a sundress with ruffled straps. The fabric's red seemed too deep for the tentative heat of May on the west coast.

Red filled Norman's vision as he sat in the crowded bus holding the baby, while Kyra stood gripping the handhold above. He looked up at her face and arms. Bony. At least the skirt hid her legs. His glance slid off to other passengers' summery bags and sandals, their bare limbs, then past the sleeping baby and down to his cast. So heavy. Wasn't there better stuff now, high-tech foam, something? Weeks of physio. Still the crutch. Walking to the bus stop with his family, he'd felt himself a prisoner attempting escape with the irons still attached.

His eyes couldn't resist looking again at Kyra. Jaw, chin, cheekbones, all hard lines. Short hair, brushed back.

It didn't dare tickle her soft earlobe.

A cramp began. With effort Norman adjusted himself so his daughter's relaxed body weighed less on his good leg, more on his arm.

Kyra said, "Don't look so put-upon. At least you've got a seat."

The baby's eyelashes, delicate.

As the bus lurched, he took another glance up. Kyra's arm stretched downward from the handhold, straight and lean to a fully exposed pit.

Norman closed his eyes.

Opened.

The stance made of her armpit a startlingly large hollow. Dark but not hairy, no no, shorn, more than shorn, chemically denuded (perhaps below the epidermis some brave follicles endured?), and dry, and deep. Rimmed by taut lumpy muscles, ligaments, something. Bones? There must be bones. That red frill, ruffle, whatever. If a person put a thumb in the pit and an index finger on the frill and squeezed, the digits might nearly meet through a band of gristle. He couldn't do it.

"What's that ugly look for? Does she need to be changed?"

"Maeve's fine, Kyra. It's just a few blocks to the beach."

"Garbage, shopping, laundry, I've been on my feet for hours already."

"You wanted this outing."

As his wife frowned anxiously at Maeve, her eyeshadow wrinkled and flakes of mascara jostled one another. Bending, she exhibited her clavicle and chest, not quite her cleavage, but the red fabric did stick out. The breasts must still be there. To touch, unimaginable. Norman winced. Pain needled his leg. He lost hold of his crutch. Maeve stirred.

"Can't you even sit still? She'll wake."

"If you had a driver's license, we could have come in the car."

"Norman, you know I don't have a good spatial sense."

"Adults do learn to drive, Kyra. Of course, some effort's required."

"It's her birthday! Can't you think about anyone but yourself?"

Turning away, she switched to the handhold across the aisle.

Maeve relaxed and happily crawled further into dream. She drew on a year of life to create peacock-blue fantasies that swirled, clouded, then broke into the gold stars her dad had shown her through the apartment window.

Norman travelled too, riding the Number Five up up and away into the brightness over English Bay, past the Planetarium and south to Pacific Spirit Park. Here the bus landed by a trailhead. Easily, he stepped off to walk into the forest smelling of warm resin, bark, earth, leaves and needles, animal scat. Nearby sounded dropping water. In all the green, the only noise. No birds. What made birds fall silent? He knew he knew, but couldn't say till he saw the little merlin on a swaying cedar branch. Her beak, such a curve! Sharp, to rip. All the other feathers in the wood folded down still, still, while she stared. At him? No, at a world hard to live in.

At the beach, Norman insisted they have their picnic by a bench.

"Why not sit on the sand, like everyone else?"

"If I go down that far I'll never get up. Is that what you want?"

"Can you at least get our lunch out? Find the bottle-opener?"

"I don't see any pickles."

"They're in the fridge. You know, in the kitchen?"

"It hurts me to walk, remember?" Norman waved his crutch.

"So. I'm to spend all afternoon trudging about with her."

They ate.

Then Maeve smiled at the sloshing noisy blue as her mother applied sunscreen to the exquisite skin. Eased the child into her yellow bathing suit. Set on a floppy hat. Kissed her.

"The water looks great. Wish I could wade!"

"Whose fault is that?"

When Kyra shed her dress, her bikini (black and white stripes, unfamiliar) enabled the sight of many knobs. Her spine, a bony snake. Did humans have three hundred bones? Two? In wrists and knees alone, dozens. Norman had broken his tibia and fibula, fibia tibula, whatever. How had he ever desired her? If he tried to remember the afternoon when they'd made Maeve (enchanting sweetness), his penis shrank.

Her cheeks shone. "I try to look nice."

With the baby in her arms, his wife walked into the ocean. A Teacup Yorkie barked angrily at the waves, and Maeve laughed.

Unable to sketch a scenario in which his wife would drown but his daughter survive, Norman turned to memories of his skiing accident. This video now slid by as if professionally directed. On the mountain. A last run, maybe the last of the season. Late afternoon, still bright, no, not too late, and just ahead something broke the smooth dim white, what, how? Lurch, tumble. Bone-crack, snowy echo.

An abandoned ski pole.

"It shouldn't have been there."

"*You* shouldn't have been there."

Kyra repelled all attempts to edit that dialogue.

Norman gritted his teeth. Tomorrow he'd be back on campus. Hours of solitude. New hearers for his tale.

Smiling, he saw on the ocean Maeve's yellow bum. Alongside floated the hat. Where was Kyra?

How did Norman stumble across the collapsing sand and wade through loud water, cursing brandishing his crutch shouting their names?

His wife stood up. God but she looked tired. Mother and baby kissed, giggled. He fell on them, full of tears. Through the wet bikini Kyra's breasts were warm. Other bathers helped them to shore, brought their gear to the curb, phoned for a taxi. The pain was huge. Maeve stopped howling.

His wife sniffled, wringing out the hat. "I *will* learn to drive."

"My leg, my fault." He patted a red frill. "It's been hard for you."

Thus they spoke, helplessly wound in and wounded by these early attempts to manage, make a meal of it, articulate the bones, marry.

Blue Clouds

OFTEN NO ONE NOTICES THE PROBLEM, the pattern till a man's in his thirties or even forties. By then he's had several—serious relationships, the comrades say. Serial monogamy, the coms say that too. If his teens were examined there'd be no surprise finding he'd favoured girlfriends with dear little sisters, but here at the hall people mostly arrive in their twenties. Their time before the movement is hidden, except what they pick to tell, and telling is cleaning.

Back up.

Such a man, when he falls for a woman she has a daughter. Maybe two. Could be sons also, but he's not aiming for importance in the life of a small man. It's the small woman he wants. Oh, not to rape, though maybe a hug she'll remember on a birthday, or when she's back from summer camp. No, he wants to implant his image, so if she thinks Man it's him. He puts his arm round her mother, tongue-kisses, turns to smile. *This is how it's done. Your mum likes this.*

An offer to babysit—heard it, seen it. Smiling, the young mum goes off to her CR group. This guy really wants her to be liberated! He plays with the little girl, helps with homework, is fun with her friends, and if she's in her teens lets her know sideways that boys haven't much to offer. He and she chat about how immature they are, she deserves better.

Then, always, he's suddenly charmed by a fresh girl/ woman combo.

Break-up, stale mother alone again, seen that too. A child who misses him can be comforted, but a teen turns sour, specially to revolutionary mum.

Exceptions, yes. Roy's a carpenter, in his late forties. On him, those years look good. He and Marion and her daughter came to Vancouver from the Calgary branch ten years ago. At the Friday suppers R and M are side by side at the big table. They dance, they picket and poster and go to conventions. Marion's a lifer at the post office, friendly, considerate. Not much for theory. Jennifer just finished high school. Hasn't joined the Youth. Comes to the Oct Rev and May Day banquets, that's all. Sullen.

I asked the old one, "Who's her dad?"

"None of your beeswax," she told me.

The true sign of no nastiness with Roy? He and Marion and Jennifer don't live together. To be under the same roof, that's what the girl-hunters plot, but this mum and her daughter keep their own place.

Enough chit-chat.

The bathrooms at the movement hall are Monday. The Youth can't manage booze, not only them either, so after every weekend there's vomit. The divided bucket has cleaning solution one side, water the other, so hot it hurts. Dip mop, use the side-press wringer, repeat. Repeat. Disinfect the wheezing toilets. Rub abrasive cream on porcelain. Shake deodorizing powder on the floor, sweep.

Done, the bathrooms don't look like ads, but they're better than the Cavalier's. Monday's next job that is, down the street. Pub washrooms take twice as long to clean. Shovel, more like. Stinking loops of paper that never reached the bowl, condoms, underpants, butts, coke, bloody pads draped over the pedal-cans, smashed glass, the red crushed wax of lipstick.

THE PROBLEM OF THE STRONG WOMEN IS DIFFERENT.

The old one's in her sixties. Pushy as hell to survive and support her girl (near forty now) and do the political. Husband? AWOL decades back, couldn't manage her. Such a life, rebelling through Depression, War, Cold War, struggling for abortion and birth control. Still at it. Startled and happy to meet today's young libbers. Hardworking beyond hardworking. Known to every lefty in the city, admired.

"No point any man sniffing around thank you very much. I like my independence."

Used to be, her typewriter rattled on for hours. Arthritis now. Hates help.

Her daughter's the opposite. When she comes round, not often, always for money, the old one's sad after. Stays a long time in a bathroom to re-braid her hair, the tiara brown still with grey woven in. Out again. Slam. "Jake, you call this sink clean?"

Marion sometimes sits with her. Quiet talk. A hug round the shoulders.

Back *up*!

Women like the old one don't mean harm. They're just big. Breathing normally, they suck out all the oxygen. Beloveds can suffocate.

Enough.

Cleaner, that's the job here at the hall. And handyman.

Why can't the TU comrades—revolutionary electricians, carpenters, fishermen, longshoremen—shim the filing cabinet, rewire the ceiling light, put a new ribbon in the Remington when the old one's fingers won't? Because they work. Or, in this period of intensifying struggle, they're on strike. Locked out. A demo, flying picket, union meeting. Weekdays, they're not here.

The men on staff, different. Before, they were students. Can't put a handle on a pencil sharpener, let alone finesse the old Gestetner. Once the present Organizer took twenty minutes by the clock fussing over whether to phone Toronto Centre long-distance. (No.) The O swivels his chair about, reads, wouldn't notice a mass uprising at the front door.

Last week the old one reamed him out when a still-meaty chicken carcass vanished from the fridge.

"There's petty cash in this hall, too," shouting. "Typewriters, easy to pawn. Open your eyes and ears, asshole!"

Back up back up *back up*.

Girl-hunters, strong women—these are *types*. Learned to identify, over two decades of cleaning here. Others too.

The too-enthusiastic contact who toils at the hall night and day for months, then ceases. No word. "Here on a visit," the coms state.

The misfits, so-called, those with a serious lack, a family it may be, looks, social ease, fluency in English, even a job. They want compensation.

So do those mourning a religion or a love. Mourning a baby, once, but after two years dying of grief she revived and left.

As for the nutcases, no one anywhere knows what to do about them. If forcibly removed in ambulances, such coms may return to throw furniture and rant.

Back *up*!

Roy too lives in the old low-rise near English Bay. The Sandringham. Good construction, not like now. Solid wood doors, brass carpet-rods on the stairs (tricky to clean), small delivery cupboards next to each apartment door. For milk, long ago. Horse-drawn cart no doubt. Roy's on the top floor. Says Hello. Chats at the mailboxes, or in the laundry near the little basement suite. In exchange for interior maintenance, reduced rent. A deal. Ideal. Once Roy wisecracked about old mole Revolution, underground. Nothing to say occurred. The place in fact is bright.

Most tenants are elderly, female, alone. Some dodder.

Not Mrs. Wolfe. That Saturday she came to me. She'd been away a day or two on Bowen, lovely weather, and now feared for Miss Nugent above her, who did not answer door or phone.

"But I heard a tap on my ceiling."

To the second floor. In Mrs. W's bare spare kitchen, listening upwards to silence.

Then to the manager's apartment. What a jeezly mess. Russell's always sozzled since his wife died, couldn't locate a key. Mrs. W's eyebrows up to the hairline.

The stairs again, third floor, seeking Roy's skill and strength. Rap rap.

Mrs. W pointing, "That milk cupboard. Could someone get through?"

Broad male shoulders the problem, not only Roy's.

He said, "I'll phone Marion. Jennifer might."

Not long after, the two arrived. The girl slender as celery. Roy broke open Miss N's milk-door.

Mrs. Wolfe's trill. "Emily! Emily?"

Nothing.

The girl's arms, head, shoulders into the aperture, Marion lifting legs to help. Jennifer's bum, compressed, wiggling through. Roy's gaze. Savouring. A tumble, a scramble. The latch clicking open.

What was expected. Not dead but cold, one hip wrongly angled. Ugly breathing. The kitchen floor puddled. Been there two days anyway, the ambulance guessed.

Miss N taken, feet first as the saying goes, return unlikely. Siren fading. Mrs. W weepy, Roy and Jennifer slipping out, useless Russell barging in.

Marion. "A cup of tea, Mrs. Wolfe? Your place? Best to take your friend's keys." Poking through the shabby purse, more tears.

Left alone to clean up, also as expected. Floor soon clear, but Roy to be all rethought. Marion too. The girl didn't arrive alone. Not allowed? Those separate apartments. How did they live in Calgary?

EACH MONDAY, THE QUALITY OF THE PREVIOUS evening's branch meeting is palpable in the hall.

Attacking the bathrooms, even a humble contact—a man who's never joined, never paid dues, invented a party-name, raised a hand, spoken his word, taken to the streets, held a banner, waved a leaflet, a man who only cleans for statutory hours as he cleans all the rental spaces in this building, offices, storage rooms, cubbies for solo notaries accountants psychics—even that man can sense last night's doings. Fear sometimes. Anger, agitation. The tang of power.

To sense.

Long long ago, a so-called friend of the mum whispered she hadn't wanted this baby. Tried to have it out, failed. Illegal then, still. This heard at thirteen, approx. Why that whisper? Mean. A child's word, and correct. Rancid with meanness. Much thought given to that. Life alone with the mum, scanty hard rough, tempers lost voices raised but never an unwanted feel, not even with the school troubles, *abc* and *xyz* and all between. She wasn't a big person, either. Plenty of air. Though large when gone.

Years later, recognition: that tale-teller's envy of the mum who had her failure by her side. Warmth ran all the way back through the shared time.

BACK UP *BACK UP*.

The hall, one morning. Like sniffing leftovers, when the nose dictates *On the turn*. Irrevocable. Trouble.

At big tables the coms fold, staple, lick stamps, smoke, say little. No printing sounds from the back room, the monster's on the fritz. This week's forum leaflet, a purplish ditto. Nobody's pleased. Papers all over the O's office, wastebasket slopping. His plaid shirt stiff with sweat. What a reek. The worker daily handling dirt grime scum cum dust rot grit mould ooze shit pee grease slime puke scuzz—fresh overalls contain his clean body.

On such a day, routine sustains. Ammonia. Baking soda. Wet-mop snaking over lino. The power of bleach. New rubber gloves. The chrome, where not pitted, shines.

Tired.

The old one, not talking, sternly brings Jake's coffee.

Not enough sugar. After twenty years she should know.

All else done at last, check the stuck Gestetner. Ink can't get through. Roller? Drum? Something inside, invisible, and no time now to take it apart.

Tired. A nap on the fold-out cot? Better to exit this bad atmosphere. The Cavalier's dirt, a relief.

LATE AFTERNOON, SAME DAY. GOING HOME.

Mrs. Wolfe outside the Chinese grocery, holding a turnip. "Jake, that Jennifer is in the building."

Clarification. Mrs. W has gone up to air out Miss N's place, launder the lonely teatowel and undies in the wicker hamper. Saw the girl.

"I've never liked that man's looks. Trouble coming."

In she goes, to pay for her vegetable.

She too sees types.

If she met the old one?

Scorn, first, for both. Prim proper, tough coarse. But they'd find links. Hard work, care for others, disapproval. Mrs. W used to be a crack typist.

Looking up at Roy's windows. That girl in his bed, bum and all. The mother alone.

Telling should have happened then, right then. A word to the old one. To the women's fraction leader, not that Ms. Loose Tits ever notices a cleaner's work. To the O, even. Should, should. Telling is cleaning, but. But she was under The Sandringham's roof, night after night. Close by.

Wake, sense her. Once, up the carpeted stairs. Silence. Moon backlighting stained glass. The corridor still, by Roy's. No vibrations.

Some days later, he's in the laundry room. Cross. Shoving sheets into the dryer.

"Nothing but meddling old women here."

The couple find somewhere else. At night, the building's different.

ON WEDNESDAY, TENSION COATS THE OFF-SMELL at the hall, tension like before a demo, or a bitter forum where everyone knows the TU coms will haul some yelling sectarian out. What though? There's been no announcement.

Kitchen today.

After the big Friday suppers it's late when the coms clean up, all are tired, the fluorescents cast distorting shadows. Mondays, bathrooms. Wednesdays: degrease. Sharp liquids force soft fats to huddle into little orbs, while hard ones slide off like scabs from counters, sinks, oven racks, shelving, baking pans, soup-kettles.

The new spray foams go where a soapy rag can't. Skin itches. Eyes sting. The old one reads aloud the cans' contents, but she's no chemist. Old cleansers are harsh too, for that matter. Over time, steel wool blurs fingerprints.

Today the sink won't drain. A wire hook fishes out carbonized macaroni stiff with tapioca cement. Still, water doesn't rush down.

Cut-off valve. Bucket. Hands and knees, j-pipe, wrench, open, scrape, but the foul blockage lacks any spoon, bottle-opener, pencil. No obvious blame.

Back painful, twisted. The Gestetner can wait.

WORK SOCKS, CHEAPEST AT ARMY & NAVY. Parcel in hand, out to sunshine, and on the corner a group of women. Not young, not libbers. The light's hard on used skin, bare arms. A chocolate bar, shared. Laughter in the sun. The old one's daughter waves her cigarette wildly in the air. More giggles, affection all round. Watching, a fellow on crutches. Once a logger? Skid row's full of broken men. Coal dust ground down into every old miner's cheeks, forehead, ears, into the eyelids' red linings.

"JENNIFER IS EIGHTEEN." THE OLD ONE SPEAKS through tight teeth. "A woman grown. Won't listen, naturally. Little fool. As for *him*." She goes on scalping potatoes.

The big machine releases the coils of its hose.

To run the vacuum is to be doubly invisible. From room to room the roaring goes, without a glance from coms rolling out paper table-covers, slinging cutlery, setting up chairs, lectern, lit table. Fridays aren't as important as Sundays, but they do matter. Suppers and forums draw contacts.

Pull the cord from one outlet, plug into another. The beast snorts up dirt.

In the noise-gaps comrades go on talking loudly as they pin up the regular decorations, posters of screaming naked child, screaming kneeling woman, man shot dead in the ear, a president's snarl, women holding sky.

Talk talk. Someone surprised those two in Stanley Park. Movement in bushes.

Not just someone. Marion. At the branch exec she made a scene.

Jennifer wouldn't listen to the old one, laughed at her mother. No, Marion slapped her daughter. True, both.

Jennifer and Roy moved the girl's stuff to his place. Every single thing.

Roy's quitting the movement. No, refused to quit. Cited women's liberation, the girl's right to control her own body, choose lovers freely.

At this the mother shouted, "Bullshit! God damn you to hell." Lots of atheists still curse by God.

The women's fraction mostly on side with the mother, two women leaders against. The O undecided. Expel Roy? Don't?

As the vacuum noses towards its cave, the old one leaves the kitchen, wades into the hissing gossip. "Shut up, the lot of you! Can't you see it's a tragedy?" Throws off her apron, blunders out weeping into summer rain.

About this handyman's work. After the vacuum's quiet, no one says, "Wow, look at the floors!"

Stocky, not young, not authoritative, not admired. Who'll observe a toilet's blanching? An unspotted mirror, shelves cleared of particles? Young coms assume things clean themselves. Telling is cleaning. Without, the slide from malfunction to breakdown, mess to filth.

Rare, to eat supper at the hall. The tables packed, loud. Who peeled the spuds after the old one left? No matter. Plain food, plentiful.

All await, none saying so, the arrival of—Roy? He'd have the nerve. Jennifer? Raging Marion?

None.

Staying to hear the speaker is beyond rare, but to leave feels incomplete. Plus disloyal to the old one still AWOL.

The draft dodger at the lectern is black Irish, his family raw from Dublin to New York somewhere in the 19th century. Witty yet dead serious. A vocabulary to stun. Vietnam his theme. His topic, divisions in the anti-war movement over slogans. With vigour he parses *Victory to the Vietcong, Bring the Troops Home, Stop Canadian Complicity, US Out Now*, arrives at the right conclusion—and leaps off to a prosecutor's summing up of capitalism's bellicose crimes. Then a paean to the Vietnamese. To the sacrifice and glory of the workers' movements around the world. Their history. Future.

When with a startled look the speaker ceases, applause. All rise spontaneously to sing the *Internationale*. He blushes, and here's the old one up the aisle, tiara damp with rain, to clap him on the back, the first of many.

Not including her daughter. When did she sneak in? The bleak face scornful of hall, speaker, song, applause. Oh why tonight, her mum happy? How to get rid? The handyman's hand to pocket too slow, the forum over, everyone in motion, and those pairs of eyes find each other.

A kind of finish?

Not yet.

To the Cavalier as a customer, alone, to think of that young man's exultation, the old one's sorrow. Days of blaming till she'll be anything like herself. If hand quicker, would all have altered? That daughter's determined to wound. So. No, this error isn't like not telling about the girl, which might have changed things.

Coward. Worse. A second beer.

The daughter's contempt targets her mother, but it's common everywhere these days, on the call-in radio shows, TV, the talk on buses. Fear of the left, loathing even.

What if no young rebelled? Just grew old?

Before departure, a visit to the men's room. Disgusting, though scrubbed savagely this morning. There's the answer to *What if*.

The dark hike down to English Bay. Will Roy's bedroom light be on? No, dirty coward. They're elsewhere.

A SUNSET.

Here on the beach at English Bay, a sharp curve in the seawall makes good shelter to watch the sky turn gold and orange. People come round that point squinting westward, don't see anyone at their feet on the sand.

Can that be Roy, hungry, hang-dog?

Be certain!

Up from beach to path, scurry ahead of the pair. Dip down by shrubs.

She's in view first. *Cat got the cream, look at me!* Not a glance at that figure by her side, desperate, starved.

Watching a handsome man thus: hot tasty spite. Meanness. Typical. The colours in the sky go on for hours.

WEEKLY, THE BISSELL BEATS AS IT SWEEPS as it cleans the carpet-runners on the first floor of The Sandringham, the second, third.

Dust the sills of the stained-glass windows, nearly colourless by day. Dust banisters.

Behind Miss N's door, silence.

Behind Roy's too.

Neither he nor Marion appears at the hall, their absence a sore licked by sixty tongues a day. Other coms take on their assignments. The O studies documents. For no reason the old one's arthritis lets up, and at 110 wpm the Remington's carriage-bell rings madly for the movement's newspaper, minutes, letters, drafts of pamphlets.

THE CAVALIER'S LINO IS SO SCARRED and broken that cleaning the floor is ritual only, but the front windows still do respond.

What? The old one's limping down the street towards the pub. Well-known of course, Red Annie, local character.

Out of the boozy dim, vinegar rag in hand.

"Jake, it's Jennifer. Get Marion."

In the struggle towards reading, some words are fireworks. *War,* for example, even if it comes up as *raw,* once learned isn't forgotten. Same with hearing. The girl's name explodes.

Run.

"Good comrade!" cries the old one.

Seven blocks downtown, hot bright streets, breathless.

At the post office, the mother's on a break. Where? Run upstairs, the cafeteria, panting, not there, down, corridors, where? Doors, counters, asking.

At last Marion's surprise, terror.

"Quick," she gasps, exiting the PO, and vinegar rag waves for a taxi.

Arrival. Marion headlong into the hall.

The cab waits.

From the Gestetner room, the O's swivel chair emerges. Slumped in it, pale Jennifer, eyes half-closed. The old one pushes the chair forward, kicks at Roy, elbows him away.

"Mummy?"

"Darling!" They embrace.

Marion grabs the chair-back, heads for the door. Roy trails.

With the old one, a shared stare at the print-room. No lovers. The Gestetner, still to be eviscerated. Ditto machine. Folded-out cot. Silkscreen. Splats on the lino.

"Later!" She pulls an arm. "They've used it for weeks. He'd got a hall key somehow." Passing the O's office.

"Damn fool never noticed."

Out to the sidewalk.

"Bastard!" The mother spits.

Roy's chin drips. "It wasn't a quack I took her to! I'd never do that, Marion, you know me! I love her."

"In we get, darling."

Taxi's off to Emergency.

The not-father-to-be runs after. "Come back!" Slows. Slinks off.

Double-quick to the Cavalier, for a mickey. A grateful swig.

Back. Into the kitchen, to the old one.

She swallows. Again.

Calmer now.

"If the cops don't come down on us for aiding and abetting, we'll be lucky. Procuring, even. Bloody irresponsible." She doesn't know the half of that. "So he quote loves her. Typical." Sighing, she swallows once more and sets the flask down, smooths her hair. Back at the Remington, she won't notice the bucket's clank. Cleaning solution this side, pink water that.

AT THE PO, MARION PUTS IN FOR A TRANSFER and returns to Calgary.

Strong Jennifer moves to Toronto. Bum never seen again.

At the next branch meeting, Roy shoves in to argue his case, shout it, till the TU coms throw him out. In this the old one doesn't exactly take pleasure, but she doesn't not either.

Russell locates the *Apt For Rent* sign, pens *2* clumsily before *Apt*.

A day later, a summons from Mrs. W.

"Jake, look what that man did before he left."

The Sandringham's garbage cans, tossed. Newsprint all over the alley, cat litter, tins, jars, peels and grounds, bacon fat, tea bags. Slimy leavings coat the cans' insides. After tomorrow's pickup, scrub. Russell won't do it. Somebody has to.

"He even threw these out." Wet white papers stick to asphalt, drift under parked cars. She holds a handful. "From when Jennifer was a little girl."

Artworks, must be back through elementary. One picture has a strip of green along the bottom, red flower-dots above, a white sky thick with paint. Along the top are plump blue clouds with scalloped edges.

"Poor girl. She got that wrong too."

This doesn't cover the whole situation, yet nothing to say occurs. Mrs. W stoops to gather up more refuse.

Red Girl Rat Boy

IN MARCIA'S FAVOURITE BOOK, Cinderella's stepsisters had thin carroty hair. So did Hansel and Gretel's mother, and the wicked fairy not invited to the christening, but Snow White's stepmother had rolling auburn curls that filled a page. They gleamed. Her image, doubled by the speaking mirror, made Marcia's insides feel hollow. She looked at it so often that the book readily fell open just there. This pleased the aunt whose gift it was.

In a magazine of Mum's, left open on the sofa, Marcia saw an ad for shampoo. Carefully, secretly, she cut out the sheet of rippling hair, mahogany-red. In her small bedroom she looked about. Where? Mum was always cleaning. Not the bookcase, though. The image slid into *Chickadee*, also from that aunt.

In time the back issues all thickened with highlights, streaks, conditioner. Always the magazines showed more blondes and brunettes, even more silvers, than redheads. Never enough.

At night, Marcia did not argue for a later bedtime. After kisses from Mum and the aunts, she used her flashlight to choose from the shelved treasures. Back under the quilt, she stroked the invisible hair, imagining colour, then slid the paper behind her bed. She remembered, every morning, to hide it again.

At school that September, for the first time the kids sat in rows.

In front of Marcia sat a new girl, down whose back cascaded red-gold hair in a shining tumble drawn in by a scrunchy. Beyond reach. When the teacher moved the class into groups the ripples came nearer, but as the weeks went by the row suited Marcia best. For hours each day, the red hung right before her. Sometimes, a ribbon. Sometimes the hair swayed, once it got past a pair of frail barrettes at the temples.

Red-girl's face was putty with small pale eyes. Irrelevant. That hair enlivened Marcia's fingers, the crevices where they met her palms, the palms themselves. Her inner wrists shivered at the nearness of the silky warmth. Mesmerizing, how the classroom's fluorescent beam bent one way on a curl's crest and another in its hollow, while a single hair, fallen, made a sleek red thread on a sleeve. Marcia's glances punctuated silent reading and subtraction and graphs, yet her hands still ached.

One day the new boy behind Marcia—he'd transferred in after Thanksgiving—abruptly signalled flu season by throwing up.

"Ewwww!"

The teacher led him away. He reminded Marcia of Hamelin's rats, though his teeth weren't so prominent. Under his lips his chin sloped right back, and his scrape of blond hair ended in a rat-tail.

Giving the janitor space to clean up the mess, the kids shoved their desks close. Now those red strands lay heaped before Marcia. Curls slid between her fingers, rode over and under knuckle and thumb as she pretended to write at the teacher's direction. As with her mother's scissors, she took care. No lift, no intrusion must be detectable. All went well until Red-girl reached for a dropped pencil. In a nanosecond Marcia let go but emitted a sound.

Smirks, grimaces nearby—these weren't about the continuing stench of pine cleanser blended with puke.

Chilled and flaming, Marcia held her own pencil tight. Her other hand grasped her seat as the gold-red swirled, bounced. Once Red-girl put her head back, laughing; the tide rolled in towards Marcia's chest and out again. When Red-girl scrubbed at her page with an eraser, the curls slid *sssshing* back and forth across Marcia's desk, inches away. *Sssssh.*

When she got home, her fingers still hurt.

Mum sniffed her. "What's that nasty smell?"

That night Marcia got a special hair-wash with Mum's own shampoo. In bed, she cried at her old ignorant pleasure in coloured paper.

Next day one aunt said, "Pity her hair's so mousy."

"Fawn," said the other. "Fawns are pretty."

Her mum sighed. "I just wish she had more friends."

"Any, you mean," said the first aunt. "She's a loner. Just like him."

"Marcia is not like him!"

Rat-boy came back to school.

As he walked down the hall, boys made vomiting noises. He made louder ones and laughed. Thus he joined the group that sneered and swaggered about the playground, tripping up kids on their way out of the portables. Every time Rat-boy went to his desk he bumped Marcia's. She didn't look up.

Marcia, invited to a birthday party, agreed to go.

"Get her hair cut, first. All those split ends."

"Long and loose suits Marcia. She's like a girl in a fairy tale."

"Hopeless!"

The mum snapped, "At least she's not obsessed with her looks, like some people."

Red-girl wasn't at the party.

A circle game was played. In darkness, mysteries passed with shrieks from hand to hand. *What is it? Guess!* Slithery spaghetti, peeled grapes. Unseen, Marcia touched the hair of the girl beside her. Stringy, dry, hateful. She wiped her fingers on her dress, then received a handful of chunked-up pomegranate, for brains.

In the birthday girl's bedroom some dolls still resided, though set aside on a shelf. No redheads. One brunette had braids all down her back, silky-soft. Marcia undid them, did them up. After the others drifted downstairs again, she found nail scissors in a bathroom. Right by the skull she cut off a braid, then hid the doll behind all the others.

Doll hair was way, way better than paper. Red was imaginable.

At school, Rat-boy and his friends squelched their armpits as girls went by, or they farted. They got into the girls' washroom to dump wastebaskets and trash the vending machines. In his newsletter to parents, the principal alluded obliquely to all this.

"Marcia, do these boys ever bother you?"

"What?"

"Can't you ever listen?" Her mum read aloud again. Marcia shrugged and went upstairs.

"Bet she has a crush." The first aunt.

"My girl's only eleven!"

"Have you forgotten what we were like?" The aunt looked from sister to sister. "Maybe you just don't want to remember."

Weeks later, the mother of the birthday-party girl surfaced.

Housecleaning, she'd exposed the mutilated toy. Her daughter said at once, "Marcia. That weirdo."

The principal and guidance counsellor showed Marcia's mum the doll. Marcia, also present, at first admitted nothing. After she gave in, the grown-ups sent her out into the hall. Rat-boy came by, saw her sullen on a bench. His eyebrows went up. He winked, raised his thumb. She stared.

"I've never been so ashamed," said the mum that evening,

One aunt laughed. "Not true!"

"You can just shut. Up."

Softly the other inquired, "Marcia, can you tell us why?"

The mum finally demanded to see *that thing*.

Soon enough she found the braid, under Marcia's mattress. The girl watched, tense, as her mother rummaged through closet and dresser but bypassed the bookshelf.

At school, the only scissors provided were short and blunt.

Marcia opened her mother's sewing basket, hesitated, replaced it. The next day, having no choice, she opened it again.

Then she waited.

Waited.

A month went by, thirty-one calendar squares for a child who beheld for hours each day, at close range, what she desired. Once, in the changeroom after gym, Red-girl stood close enough for Marcia to smell her hair.

Rat-boy now bumped Marcia's desk hard. If she tucked her feet under her chair, he'd stick his forward to kick her. Once he waited on a street corner near the school and tried to walk alongside. When she paid no attention, he followed her.

The mum said, "Marcia seems much better now, doesn't she?"

"Didn't you get that wake-up call? A dangerous age she's going into. As you should know."

The second aunt, "Marcia's imaginative. Creative."

"She makes things up! And those fairy tale books encourage her."

The mum stated, "My little girl does not tell lies, and you needn't remind me what I did as a teenager. You did plenty yourself."

"Aren't you at all worried?"

"Marcia's fine."

"Yeah, fine. And yes I did, but I didn't get caught. Not many single mums have your support system, either."

"Another reminder I don't need!"

"What about love? No one's mentioned love."

The mum looked down. The first aunt rolled her eyes.

"Don't you remember wanting, wanting till your heart hurt?"

Marcia's mum couldn't find her sewing scissors, made inquiries. Annoyed at her own carelessness, she had to make do with kitchen shears.

During the monthly school assemblies, Marcia's class sat cross-legged on the floor at the back of the gym. Rat-boy was behind her at November's gathering, she right behind Red-girl. All three sat far from the teacher, who aimed a warning look at Rat-boy on turning to inspect her class.

The autumn-leaf hair gleamed.

Announcements. A skit from Grade Two, a song from Kindergarten. Applause for Grade Seven's track-and-fielders' success at city-wide.

As always, the program ended with the principal.

When everyone clapped after his first joke, Marcia's nerve broke. Her shaking hand wouldn't leave her pocket.

In the second outburst of applause she didn't even try.

As the speaker neared his final punchline, she remembered that fairy tales offered three chances. Only three. Grasping a tress of red silk, she raised the open blades as the laughing girl flung her head back hard and Rat-boy reached to grab Marcia where her breasts would have been if she'd had any.

Time, many people said.

Give it time. Give her time.

Just let time pass. Which it did, though not because anyone let it.

Red-girl never came back to school. Rat-boy got transferred out.

Marcia's mother, vacuuming, nudged her daughter's bookshelf so magazines fell and released their hoard.

"A blizzard of paper," she wept to her sisters, "a blizzard. Why?"

"The girl was plain, I'm told," said one aunt. "So it was love."

The other's expression said *Slut.* "You burned it all, right?"

"But why?"

A decade later, her mother's question stayed with Marcia.

Often her desire was water not wine, skim not cream, and after sex there swelled a sense of insufficiency. Hair colour, its brilliance and fire, didn't change that. She refused or excused herself from more love-making, left whatever bed she'd got herself into and went off elsewhere, over the hills and far away and still with that hollow inside.

The Sister-in-Law

THAT WINTER THE SISTER-IN-LAW EMAILED to say she was coming to the city. The siblings hadn't seen her for eight years, since the funeral. Their brother Alan had died driving a rental car in Albuquerque. So—was Olivia still related to them?

The sister, phoning her extant brother, scoffed. "That woman made Alan go to the States. And he crashed." *Post hoc ergo propter hoc,* for her, had sundered the link earlier corroded by dislike. "Void," she tested, "invalid."

He looked towards the mountains. Rain came across the water.

Also, Joyce noted, the couple hadn't been happy for some time before his death. Alan had mentioned divorce, to them though not to their mother, then still alive barely. So wasn't the sister-in-law only technically a widow?

"If there'd been children," she argued, "it'd be different. Children change everything."

Olivia's email proposed a get-together *for lunch? drinks?? dinner??? Wherever you like, I don't know Vancouver any more!!!* A smiling emoticon.

"Where'd she find my email address? Yours, for that matter?"

The brother shrugged. If Joyce would only shut up, he could brush Sadie and make his tea.

"Ronald, why can't you talk like a normal human? We'll discuss Olivia tonight." Snap.

Quiet.

Sadie gazed at him, her plumy tail just moving. As he reached to a drawer, she jumped onto the appointed stool. First he brushed her coarse outer coat. Good— but soon impatience showed. Amused, he started on her silky under-fur. Sadie squirmed with pleasure. When she'd had enough she bounced down, drank, got into her crate, twirled round and went to sleep. *The Sheltie-Pom is not available.*

While the smoky leaves brewed, Ronald imagined Alan's death, as he'd done for months after the event. The fantasy had blurred. His brother's habit of speeding, though, was hard fact. He'd got tickets, made their mother cry.

Ronald himself didn't feel like a widower, but then he'd never felt much like a husband. Or had he? Louisa. A short marriage, ended decades ago by her death. Louisa.

The timer sounded. Ronald drank, looking out at the silver Pacific, at mountain peaks swathed in cloud. Soft weather, yet every year people drowned here, or they slid off cliffs and died. *They never learn* was said, illogically, for it couldn't be the same victims every time.

Olivia still sent a card every Christmas. Elves, glitter. Ronald supposed that the university's card he mailed to her was in comparison somewhat austere.

"NO, I'LL CUT THE PIZZA," JOYCE SAID. "Classic first-born, super-responsible. Help Mum. Calm down Dad. Take care of my little brother." She sawed through to the cardboard.

"When did you take care of me?"

"*Alan.* You could always cope, Ronnie. You had a childhood. I didn't. Then Stanley's father came along, and Stanley was born. Hah!"

The two were chewing before Joyce's silent TV, where one well-dressed man shook his fist at another. The text read *Elder abuse rampant, no govt accountability.*

Ronald pulled the hard rim off his slice, as inedible. "But you and Harris were together a long time before Stanley was born."

"Don't remind me. Thirteen years. Harris was as much trouble as any kid, too." She glanced at the TV. "God, who'd go into social work?"

"I didn't see a lot of Harris. University, grad school, I was busy."

"You didn't miss much."

The door to Stanley's room was closed. No light showed.

"Will he want some?"

"Stanley does like pepperoni. Uncle Ronnie's here!" shouted Joyce, pushing aside much of the remaining pizza. Her voice cracked. "His father wouldn't have asked that. He'd just eat it all. Stanley!"

A plastic cuplet in the pizza box brimmed with a creamy substance. Hopeful, Ronald dipped his crust into it.

"They never send enough of that," Joyce said. "When our son *clearly* needed professional help, Harris wouldn't discuss it. Let alone budget for it. Or take him to his appointments."

Stanley peeped out at the food. "Is there some other uncle I don't know about, Mum?" Bearish, he shuffled forward.

Ronald, who'd not had a sighting in some time, noted his nephew's belly and drooped posture. At twenty-one, the kid looked forty. When did he shave last? Stanley's bedroom door stood ajar. On the Xbox, monstrous black-browed men all girt in white had at each other with swords.

Joyce got to her feet. The comfy chair, another channel, fresh coffee?

"No, Mum." He licked out the cuplet of dipping sauce. "I mean, Uncle Alan died, right?" His plate laden, her son disappeared.

Ronald fetched another beer for his sister. "Joyce, there has to be better pizza than this on Commercial Drive. Next month let's try somewhere else."

"You know, my benefits don't nearly cover his therapy. Where the hell is our so-called union? Social workers never fight for themselves."

"Is therapy helping him, do you think?"

She slammed the bottle down. "You think Stanley's a loser! That he's lazy and screwing me around to avoid school or work. You're wrong," Joyce croaked. "You don't know anything about depression. Stanley was devastated by Alan's death." She headed to the bathroom.

Ronald calculated. When Alan and the then sister-in-law left Vancouver for his job at an eastern university, Stanley had been four.

On the TV, a woman wept by a house with *For Sale* and *Happy Day Daycare* signs outside. The crawler read *2 Tots Shaken, In ICU.*

A knock at the door. Joyce went, crossly. A vague female muttering sounded.

"Not again! You never learn, do you?"

Footsteps went down the hall.

Ronald watched a silent commercial for Febreze and one for Dove.

Joyce came back. "She can't figure out the dryer. Twenty times I've told her, shown her. Why haven't you finished your pizza?"

"What about Olivia?"

His sister frowned. "You *still* haven't decided?"

Fetching her laptop, she found the email, hit Reply, and typed so fast the words vanished almost before Ronald read them.

Unfortunately I'll be out of town at a convention. Enjoy your visit. Joyce.

"Easy peasy!"

Seconds later their sister-in-law, if she was that, responded.

Exciting! Where are you off to?

Sister and brother gasped.

"Creepy!"

"It's as if she were waiting for us."

Joyce snorted, deleted. "Do as you please, Ronald. No skin off my nose."

On leaving her apartment, he flung into the building's dumpster the leftovers she'd insisted on bagging up for "the dog."

Driving home calmed him.

So did taking Sadie out for her last pee. The lamplit walkway behind his building skirted the enormous park, and once past a towering laurel hedge the dog and man moved through damp green semi-darkness, rooty-smelling, wildish. They started across the heronry. Leafless trees held nests in their upper branches, at the ready for next month's great arrival. Even from sixty feet below, the bowls of sticks looked huge against the sky.

In long-ago childhood summers when his brother went away, Ronald could, though he didn't often, invite friends over. His parents weren't whispering behind doors. No one cried (he meant Mum). His sister, teaching squash and golf, wasn't often home to hector. The medicine cabinet held Aspirin, cough syrup. What kind of camp accepted teenagers on antidepressants?

Nor had he been sorry when Alan and Olivia moved away. His sister-in-law had pretty hair, was pleasant, but had read nothing. Nothing. A featherhead, whose voice rose at the ends of declarative sentences. She was nice to their mother, and to their father in his decay, but a family dinner with Alan at the table was just work, done for Mum. Thank heaven she'd died first.

Now a scuttle, a rush in bushes near the path. Dog and man alert, sniffing.

No, not skunk. Coyote? Too small. Raccoon, or big rat.

Ronald gripped Sadie's leash (her hybrid could be assertively protective) and pulled her along towards the tennis courts.

Olivia's email—the punctuation so characteristic, also the smiley-face. Always a tendency to cuteness, to paper napkins printed with kittens or ladybugs, yet this sister-in-law had endured years with Alan and successfully run a small mail-order business. Perhaps still did?

Sweet box scented the air by the front steps. Spring, soon. Reading week, thus some free time. Altogether there seemed no reason not to see the putative sister-in-law.

After Sadie went to sleep in her crate, Ronald considered. Lunch would be best, a commitment less dismissive than drinks but reliably shorter than dinner. He reserved at a not unfashionable Yaletown bistro that served a fish soup he liked, and emailed Olivia. As he was about to close his computer, her exclamations arrived.

Is she always online?

In the stillness of his study Ronald gazed at his books, erect with others on the tradition of courtly love. Many academics displayed their own titles separately, but his were in with the rest, alphabetical by author. His took up most of a shelf, though.

The engineering school at that New Mexico university had courted Alan. There, would his brother have been not depressed? To Ronald, a degree-granting institution lacking medieval studies was incomplete.

Going down the hall to bed, he touched the frame of a Japanese print, a heron standing by water. For some years Louisa's photo had hung there. Where had he put it?

RONALD TURNED OFF HIS CELLPHONE at lunch, to concentrate on the situation before him.

After the goodbyes he walked quietly in the clear winter sunshine, nearly home, before opening his phone. At once it rang.

"I've called you three times! What was it like?"

"They've taken that chowder off the menu."

"Ron-*nie!*"

"She looks very well," slowly.

"Did she stick you with the bill? What was she w—"

"Olivia was sorry not to see you."

"Yeah sure."

The sun on English Bay was brassy, almost hurtful. He ended the call.

Standing at his own front door, Ronald heard silence. His stomach clenched. Then came Sadie's bark. In relief he closed his eyes. The dog ran ecstatic spirals about the hall while he gathered her leash and a poop bag. All the way down seventeen floors, she squealed with delight.

What to tell Joyce? The word *husband* wasn't used, yet clearly this Thomas, solid and prosperous, belonged to Olivia. He enjoyed the wine, savoured each fat mussel as if it were the best ever, and emptied his cone of frites except for two she accepted. He beamed at her.

"Isn't this delicious?" She ate a salad and drank San Pellegrino. Her hair was silver, still pretty, well-cut.

Thomas spooned up icky-sticky toffee pudding while he described their recent Hawaiian holiday and new bamboo floors.

A trade show had brought the pair to Vancouver. "Going great," affably. "Selling's what I do best. Used to be in toilets, before that window-coverings. I just switched up to Olivia!" He kissed her hand.

"He's made such a difference, Ronald."

"Honey, your company was doing great. I only nudged a bit."

To his surprise, Ronald would have welcomed details, but just then Olivia exclaimed about the yachts in the Creek. Her speech habits hadn't changed. Thomas responded to her enthusiasm, and over coffee he took up the bill with élan.

A hell of a lot better, for her.

Thomas's handshake felt warm. "Great restaurants you've got here, Ron. We aim to try as many as we can."

Done.

Now the elevator door opened to a lobby full of light.

Ronald jogged towards the beach, Sadie trotting alongside so fast her legs twinkled.

Thomas must have found our addresses. Or his secretary did.

At the tideline lay shards of ice, strewn with sand and seaweed, glistening in the sun.

Would Olivia have brought her man along if Joyce had come to lunch? Ronald struggled to picture his sister facing Thomas.

The dog found a dead crab and attacked.

"Not now!"

She insisted on dealing with her prey, though the wind fanned her fur so that her pink skin was visible.

"Some dogs agree to wear jackets," Ronald pointed out. He himself felt chilly when they resumed walking.

After the trek to Second Beach and round Lost Lagoon to bark at the incurious swans, then back to English Bay, the ice had melted. The crab was gone too. Once sure of that, Sadie bustled home contented.

"HELLO."

"Oh Joyce you're back early from your convention?"

"No."

"Oh, I was just going to leave a message, say Hi to you and Stanley, but if? Could I? It's years since I've seen him?"

Looking at the sofa where her boy snored, such a beautiful baby he'd been, Joyce ground her teeth.

Shortly she phoned her brother, who was about to record a program on the later pre-Raphaelites. "Just like her to sneak up on me."

"Why'd you answer the phone?" Why did he?

"Because it'll be the college or the shrink or the group-therapy guy about something Stanley's done, hasn't done, correction, I should *make* him do. Or my unit manager, asking what day it is. I have to. You know that."

"I've told you I'd stay with Stanley for a bit, give you a break."

"I hardly even play golf. You know that too."

"Are you going to take care of him your whole life?"

Ronald hadn't intended to ask that. Had Joyce even heard? His phone didn't ring angrily.

Without stopping, Sadie went by to her food dish.

He reached for the remote.

SADIE SNIFFED THE GUEST'S SHOES. Ronald nearly said, "She can be shy," when the tail began to wag.

"Oh, what a sweetie!" Sadie permitted ear-pulls, followed Olivia to the living room and sat nearby.

"Such a view! So misty by the Lagoon, the trees half gone? Like those Asian scroll things, you know?"

He brought in coffee.

"So fresh! Lovely. I loved that lunch, Ronald, didn't you? I'm glad to see you alone, though." She sipped. "I need to say, about my mistake? I tried to make your brother happy."

Alarmed, he pushed the biscotti towards her.

"Alan did love me, at first anyway, and I just thought *Here's this wonderful man but he's so sad. I'll change that!* Impossible." Her silver hair hung like a bell. "You can't make someone anything."

"It wasn't your fault."

"Your family, so intellectual. The dictionary at the dinner table? On and on about poems? Analyzing. Alan hadn't ever seen real movies, just those Bergman things? He didn't know how to have fun."

"Joyce isn't intellectual."

"No, I was so surprised when she and Harris got married? He didn't play golf or tennis or anything. Brave, both of them. But I talked to your mum before she died? Well of course before, that's the sort of thing Alan got mad at me for. She understood. She thought I should leave him."

Sadie nosed Olivia's knee.

"Is this okay for her?" She held the smallest biscotto.

Instead Ronald opened a drawer in the coffee table to get Sadie's treats. The dog gave an offended look but delicately nipped the tidbit from Olivia's fingers and flung it up in the air, to catch.

"Clever girl!"

"It wasn't your fault." Can't we go on now, the weather, her impressions of a changed Vancouver, anything?

"Instead Alan left me. That's why Albuquerque. He wanted a fresh start, you know? Then the crash? Oh, I felt *so bad.*"

"He always drove too fast."

"I even wondered, suicide?" Olivia shook her bell as if surprised at herself. By her feet Sadie lay couchant, guardian.

Ronald did not say that he believed Alan had had far too high an opinion of himself to deprive the world of his presence.

"When I met Thomas," tenderly, "he helped me. Contacted the police, troopers, whatever they have in New Mexico. No problem, oh that reminds me, flowers for Joyce of course but Stanley? Does he like movies?"

"What did the authorities say?"

"Oh, they had photocopies, *the officer attending?* It wasn't all Alan's fault. The point is, we can't *be* for another person?"

Sadie rested her head on Olivia's ankle.

"Japanese. Maybe martial arts."

Guessing thus made Ronald dizzy. He'd never carried flowers to Joyce, nor invited Stanley to a theatre, nor assessed Harris's character. He and his sister, after their brother's death, had pursued no inquiries.

"Don't you just love sushi, except the eels? Fascinating! But I must go, Ronald. The booth, Thomas."

Later he discovered her glove in the hall. Such small hands. Heavy rain began.

After half an hour in the park, man and dog were soaking, but Sadie still yanked at her leash, determined to revisit the shrubbery where that scuffle had occurred. Leaves and branches resisted Ronald. When he got through, Sadie was inspecting a rat. She looked up, proved right. The animal's eyes were gone, its stomach and haunches torn. The fur inside its ears looked soft.

At home, Ronald towelled the dog off, dried his own hair and put on his dressing gown. "Nap-time, Sadie."

But at the heron he turned the other way, to his computer.

The trade show's website sparkled with the colours of cocktail stirrers, name tags, matchbooks (who still uses those?), iPhone cases, napkins, swags of ribbon. Among the exhibitors was *Olivia's Greetings*. Each card bore her printed signature, the handwriting legible if not distinctive. So many festivities to grace each month and year, so many special birthdays.

On the way to his nap, he remembered that his parents, especially his mother, had been very fond of Louisa.

"OH JOYCE, YOU LOOK WELL!" OLIVIA CAME IN. "Your place is exactly how I remember it!"

"Why wouldn't it be? There's no money to renovate."

"For you."

Joyce took the blue irises. "You want coffee or something?"

The two women gazed at Stanley on the living room sofa. Silent, the Weather Channel showed a blizzard moving from the American Midwest towards the eastern seaboard, as far north as Nova Scotia.

Joyce went over to turn off the TV. "Sometimes that does it. Sit up, son." He stirred, releasing unwashed-body odour, stretched and closed his eyes.

His mother returned to the kitchen area.

"So much like Alan, amazing!"

"Stanley's father never liked hearing that. Made him feel quote invisible." Joyce shook instant into mugs, touched the kettle, made an *It'll do* face, poured. "Powdered's here. Sugar."

With her drink, Olivia moved towards Stanley.

Joyce found an old mayo jar and ran water. As she stuffed the irises in, one fell. She bent to retrieve it. Deep in each petal's throat ran an irregular golden streak.

A knock at the door.

"Always something." Joyce went. "Oh no, not again!"

Some minutes later she walked back into the apartment saying, "Some people never learn. They get told and told but it doesn't sink in."

Murmurs came from the sofa, then Stanley laughed.

Joyce reached the living room area just as Olivia, giggling, set a pile of DVDs on Stanley's stomach. He started reading the cover copy on one as Joyce grabbed another.

"Cartoons, little girls, what the hell, Olivia? D'you think time stands still?"

"Miyazaki, Joyce! Lovely stories. The animals only look scary? And all the kids get brave."

Reading, grinning, Stanley rose. He snatched the DVD from his mother and went to his room. Joyce took a few steps after him, stopped.

When she turned, Olivia was gathering up her things.

"I'd better go? Thank you, Joyce." She put her coffee mug on the kitchen counter. It was empty, her hostess saw, except for some milky goo at the bottom.

To watch Olivia disappear, Joyce picked up the irises again and carried them over to the window, where she set the jar on the sill.

At first the sister-in-law moved slowly along the sidewalk, several times raising her face to feel the raindrops. Then she speeded up, but not to the corner where the taxis shot by in yellow blurts. Instead she darted under the red awning of a restaurant, Italian, fancy, newly opened.

Joyce hesitated.

Hesitated.

Thrashed into her old winter coat and left the apartment.

RONALD BECAME AWARE OF SADIE in the living room. Not napping. Slobbering. At her crate, he knelt to peer and feel inside.

Grrr.

His hand met Olivia's glove. Her favour was damp, the leather pocked by teeth. He held on to it, held against Sadie's pull. Growling again, the dog let go and withdrew to the rear of her private space, where she lay down with her back to him.

Ronald too lay down, curled on the silk carpet purchased in Istanbul on his last sabbatical.

Why had he never invited Joyce out for a really good Italian dinner? He held his knees and tried to control his breathing, urgent, wildish. Was Harris still extant? Did Stanley ever see his dad? Why had Ronald himself so rarely visited his own (demented) father?

Olivia had sent the old man cards, which he saved. After his death, Joyce got cross because their mother wouldn't throw them out right away. But now they weren't children any more, not rivalrous children to say *Serve you right* when a playmate tears her knee, when a brother dies.

"Louisa," he sobbed, "darling Louisa."

Sadie emerged to stand by Ronald. She sniffed at his crotch and then his ear, licked his wet cheek. He gave her the glove.

Care

The Boss Lady in her tailored suit knelt before Bed 2's assigned closet and scuffed things off its floor as a dog scuffs up dirt, backwards. Out shot gauze rolls, bottles of body wash, packs of Depends, the Rec Director's clicker for locked wards, sunglasses, a pashmina, jigsaw bits.

Bed 2's occupant, The Wanderer, wasn't around.

In Bed 1 lay silent Teevee-gal, unpicking her sheet's hem while staring at a dark screen. Her remote was out of reach.

The Boss Lady tossed Tim Hortons cups, lipsticks, grumpy-baby photos, tiny flags, a driver's license, Tylenol, lumps of hard porridge, a blue folder, shampoo.

Grabbing that folder, she rose, and did not stop to wipe the angry tears but strode towards the door of 17-B where small brown care aides and LPNs clustered.

"You idiots didn't notice this garbage? Clean it up. That woman must go."

Stilettos carried the Boss Lady away.

The Wanderer just then was at work on a cash machine in the care home's basement. Once she'd jammed it. Not tonight, but the deposit envelopes went into her wheelchair's basket, and in the caf she scored a Danish and a banana before *Hey you!* sounded. Quickly she *whir-whirred* to the hall by the service elevator used to excrete corpses, dirty dishes, waste. She ate, waiting till she figured the care aides had finished with all the others and would be too tired to fuss.

She tossed the peel onto the floor.

HOW FRIDAY BEGAN FOR SALLY, LORRAINE, ANNABEL

All night the summer air had wafted into 17-A, sweet air, for the dumpsters below the window held only a day's load, yet unable fully to refresh the room. By the big containers a coyote sidled, sniffing, while raccoons waddled across the parking lot towards their tree-homes. Birds conversed.

The old white women lay quiet.

One was having a bowel movement.

One thought again, *The aides could just heave me out that window when I die.*

The third dreamed of a boy in a photo album.

Soon crows began to curse. Phones rang, trolleys clunked, and old Mr. Chang traversed the floor at a rate of six round trips per hour.

Pushing a trolley bearing sanitizer, tissues, lotions, wipes, Lily arrived in 17-A. Snapped on fluorescents, clashed curtain-rings, poked the nearest resident.

"Turn over, Sally."

"Mrs. Knox to you, fucking clumsy! Watch my jigsaw."

Sally's bloated body didn't resist, though, and her shit (the workday's first stink) was neatly formed. In a fresh diaper, the resident snoozed again.

Lorraine assessed Lily's steps for irritability.

"Good morning!"

"Everything late already." The aide jabbed a button. Lorraine's bed angled up, pinching her spine. "No fun for you today. Transfusion."

"Please, save my menus?"

Lily yanked Lorraine's bedside drawer open, flapped at the sheets of *Creamy Veg Potage, Garden Pasta, Vanilla Delight*. "Too many already."

"Please?"

"You, you wait for Transfer." She crossed to the third resident's bed. "No games today, Annabel. Behave! Or Boss Lady throw you out too."

"Who *too*?"

"Wanderer."

Annabel gaped.

Lorraine managed, "Where on earth could she go?"

Annabel kicked the aide, whose cry woke Sally.

Then Lily wrangled the flailing Annabel into her wheelchair. The resident scooted to the toilet, pulling herself by banging her heels, scooted back. Next her nightie got dragged off, underpants and camisole on, while she struggled, giggling. Resisted arms into blouse. Undid her skirt's Velcro.

"Score!"

Lily bent close, whispered. "Your brother, he's wait for you." Closer. "Take you out, breakfast treat, Canada Day!"

"Eric's here?"

"Dining room."

Annabel grabbed the Velcro.

"Stupid!" Sally.

"Don't believe her!" Lorraine.

Ninety-five pounds and years, her hair a thick silver crown, Annabel scooted out, her heels so keratinous they sounded *tak-tak-tak*.

Across the hall, a TV blared. *In the criminal justice system the people are represented by two separate, but equally important, groups: the police, who. . .*

Whir whir, the Wanderer's chair.

Clack clack of stilettos. "Hey you! Thief, *and* dangerous driver. You've been expelled before. Don't think it can't happen here."

Then to Teevee-gal, shouting, "I said, *Keep the volume down!*"

Next across the hall to 17-A, shoving at Lily's trolley. "How many times have I told you, *Don't leave supplies by an open door!*" She brandished a litre of surface cleanser, ivory in her black hand. "Do you speak English?"

Stone-faced, Lily exited 17-A and waited for Josie, another aide, to accompany her into Mr. Chang's room. Its other resident, Big Man, attacked staff.

"Remember," the Boss Lady told Sally and Lorraine, "these people keep you alive. I want no complaints."

Transfer arrived.

SALLY'S BUSY MORNING

Maybe there'd be pancakes for breakfast?

Waiting. Calendar, meanwhile.

Always she ticked off the weekday Activities—Mon *Bingo*, Tues *News & Views*, Wed *Crafts*, Thurs *Flower Arranging*—not that she attended. I like to relax. By Fri *Baking*, no tick appeared. Thought so! Canada Day tomorrow. Can't fool me, Lily. Turning the page, she examined the photo of July fireworks at English Bay. Pretty. Was I there once?

Waiting, she fiddled with her sunflower jigsaw.

Whir whir, an electric chair rolling in. That heavy old woman. Feet, gone. Face creased, a softening gourd.

"Not here, no. You live with Teevee-gal in 17-B. Bee bee bee!"

The Wanderer snatched at Van Gogh, wheeled to the window and threw a piece out, looked excitedly at Sally, threw another.

"Stop, I'll tell!"

The visitor U-turned and yanked the privacy curtain round Sally's bed.

"Pull that back!"

Invisibly the wheelchair departed. Sally rang her buzzer, rang. In time, hunger changed her priorities. "Where's my damn breakfast?"

With the cold food came extra Aunt Jemima.

As Sally ate, 17-B roared again. *The police who investigate crime, and the district attorneys who prosecute the offenders. These are their sto. . .*

Sally watched the doorway. Who's got her remote this time? TV's all Teevee-gal has. I hate Lily. Why don't Melia or Josie tell her off? Roberto? She licked her plate.

Nap-time.

More waiting, jigsaw.

Moving pieces fruitlessly, Sally recalled again Lorraine's saying, "The others are younger. From the same island, same village even. They can't make her do a thing."

To physio next, heavy on the walker, escorted by the aide. En route, Boss Lady.

"Lily was mean to Annabel!"

"Lies. I've no time for this."

Sally said to Lily five times, "I told on you! I did!"

So far. Then many exercises. Too many. So much bending. Knees sore. Back sore. Never a snack.

Back in 17-A at last, Sally said, "You've twisted this walker, Lily."

"Ten times maintenance fix for you."

"Fucking did not!"

Lily knocked Van Gogh bits off the table, took the mobility aid and left.

Sally couldn't find her picker-upper.

Chicken noodle, maybe? How can Annabel love that stupid brother? He never visits. Is he dead? Crackers. Apricot yogurt. One brownie, never ever two. Why'd she throw out my puzzle? Throw out Lily! The Boss Lady'd be so mad.

ANNABEL'S EXPLORATIONS

Usually in the mornings Annabel scooted to visit friends. Not today. Alone in 17-A's corridor, she hunched in her chair, whimpering *Eric, Eric.* She thumbed an old *Canadian Living*, its cover a cake resplendent with piped cream. Dozed.

A nurse cruised by, to check on this resident's psoriasis.

Tired from weeping, Annabel slept again, even when Julio arrived. He came from Lily's island though not her village. After dry-mopping 17-A for the thirty-seven seconds availed him by the institution's short-staffing, Julio dragged out the garbage bag swollen each and every day with plastic and paper opaque, clear, printed, stretchy, squashy, hard, infected, crackly, sticky, inky, fuzzy, torn, unused, wet, shit- or food- or coffee- or puke- or lipstick- or snot-stained, perfumed, precious; laden also with glass bottles, squeeze bottles, jars, tubes, tubs, ampoules, aerosols, Styrofoam and tins, empty, full, necessary, scorned. He missed the Van Gogh bits.

The sack scraped over the floor. Annabel's dreams dislimned, and as Mr. Chang wheeled by she woke. They smiled. Julio didn't.

What about lunch? Not dining-room, not after howling for Eric there, but yesterday she'd scored loonies from petty cash. So. Basement. Vending machines.

From 17-B the lawyers blared *Objection, your honour! Withdrawn. My colleague would have you believe. . .*

Lily emerged, with Teevee-gal's remote.

Annabel *tak-takked* after her, mouthing, "Tattletale! Ass-licker!"

The Wanderer, at the cash machine again, nodded.

Eating barbecue chips and a Mars bar, Annabel watched the nimble thick fingers till the Wanderer shrugged, quit.

"What's in your basket today?"

Under a ratty cardigan lay Windex, instant coffee, jelly beans, rolls of TP.

Annabel laughed. "Let's go!"

Smiling, the Wanderer unlocked a utility closet.

Their baskets soon loaded, the women wheeled to a washroom where they filled a toilet-tank to overflowing with bottles of Javex and Pine-Sol. Using packaged rags, they blocked the paper-towel feed. Although the tampon machine defeated them, they easily squirted out all the liquid soaps.

In the corridor again, they saw doctors approaching. The women stilled, heads sank to chests, eyelids drooped. Annabel's knees flopped apart. Her tongue protruded.

After the talking white-coats passed, she suggested, "Home now?" But the Wanderer rolled away, wet wheels hissing as she headed for Delivery.

Near the great door, Annabel slowed. She hadn't exited the building since ninety, but the Wanderer rolled right out.

No one there. Under a dumpster, a darting rat. Two. The women laughed at them, at the sun's warmth, the fresh air whose garbage tang included none of the chemicals used indoors to mask decay.

Now the Wanderer's heavy arms mimed throwing towards the dumpsters. Huge throws. Her body jerked, her footless legs waved.

"What?" Annabel turned back.

Sighing, the Wanderer re-entered.

On their floor, many residents were still at lunch.

In one room the Wanderer chose a watch with a green strap, *Vogue*, moisturizer, a BC Ferries ballpoint pen on which a tiny boat slid up and down. She mimed towards Annabel, who shook her head. A room emptied by death was different; she'd pick out jewellery, photos of grandsons. Treats for Eric, canned nuts, foot rub, jam.

Now the Wanderer's cardigan bulged. She looked about, intuiting, Annabel knew, today's right site. Keys bloated her fanny pack. Rumour said the Wanderer slept with it latched round her belly, gripped it even when bathed. The boiler room? That fat monster scared Annabel. No! Happily *tak-tak* followed *whir-whir* as the chairs sped past Mr. Chang, the nurses' station, dining area, kitchen, to the linen room with its towers of dry scalded sheets, face cloths, gowns, robes, towels, pads, pillowcases, coverlets, bibs.

In one wall, a square of steel. Annabel pulled the handle, and the Wanderer dumped her basket's contents down the chute.

LORRAINE, DOING TIME ALL DAY

Transfer was today embodied by Lily's second cousin Felipe, a.k.a. Hot Wheels.

Soon after he'd started at the care home, Big Man's picker-upper tripped him. The Boss Lady ordered X-rays, a union rep sympathized. Felipe was fine, but corridor 17 made him nervous. To be done with it, he came early. No breakfast didn't matter to Lorraine, yet his arrival typified time served in care: rush rush, or so slow that rage beckoned.

Once, Lorraine's transfusions came months apart. She'd spent her days in the garden (the fountain, the fountain!) or the library, and enjoyed meals at a lively table where everyone had their marbles. Now fortnightly she was shunted through a tunnel to the hospital, to be topped up with blood. The process granted little vigour. She felt, afterwards—not better, though, with her body chemistry so out of whack, naming sensations was hard.

The gurney moved.

Do names matter? If only I could read my file.

After *good morning* to Mr. Chang, Felipe hung a left, then paused to flirt at the nurses' station.

Shelves just inside its open door held the residents' blue files, thick as encyclopedias, the spines hand-lettered. Lorraine's fingers yearned as she saw her own name, Sally's, Annabel's.

The Wanderer drew up alongside. She touched Lorraine's hand, goggled urgently at her, the folders, her.

"I can't reach."

Clack clack of stilettos. Hot Wheels jumped.

The Boss Lady fingered a blue folder. "Con-fi-den-tial," softly. "Au-thor-ized rea-ders on-ly. Big words? *Close that door!*"

The nurse whimpered, the gurney shot forward.

Down down went Felipe and Lorraine.

Through.

Up up.

For hours she lay alone, watching one red plastic pouch and another shrink from fat to flaccid. Her bedsores hurt. Unless her roommates kept today's menus, June would be incomplete. And—her cellphone forgotten by her bed. Why care? I don't answer. But if I wanted. . . I told everyone, *Don't call, don't come.*

Also forgotten, her picture book of water gardens.

Going dotty? Shall I unpick hems like Teevee-gal, eat threads?

Enough.

Lily. What to do?

Soon after Lorraine came to 17-A, she'd learned how a former roommate, suffering from a migraine, asked for a cold cloth on her forehead. Wrapped in the chilly white was a turd.

"Lily just said, *Not me*." Sally snorted. "The Boss Lady didn't do a fucking thing."

"Ketchup packets," Annabel giggled. "We squished them anywhere Lily'd touch. Handles, trays. Switches. Messy!"

Now the aide put tissues and eye drops out of reach, opened the window when asked not to. "Fresh air, you smelly in here!" Laughing, she "forgot" to close the door when bathing Sally, who cried in shame. Meticulously the Laundry Lady filed 17-A's garments, yet Lily claimed favourites were MIA. Hampered by mobility aids and failing sight, the women must wait to retrieve crumpled dresses from the closet floor till Melia Josie Roberto Angelique came on shift.

Without the aides, we'd die even sooner.

The second blood-bag and time and energy drained away. At last gentle Melia came, who knew Lily's little Alicia back home.

As the gurney passed the Boss Lady's office, Lorraine glimpsed the woman head-in-hands at her desk.

Next, a gossip at the nurses' station. Oh, how long? In any bed, I'd die happy.

Finally, Van Buren's and McCoy's directives. *Get a subpoena. Get a grand jury. Get on it, gentlemen, get going.*

Delivered into 17-A, Lorraine saw that her cellphone was gone.

FRIDAY EVENING: PLANNING

KD in foil-lidded Styrofoam. Yucky coleslaw, and Sally ate all three servings. Canned mandarins. Lorraine gave hers to Annabel, chocolate milk to Sally.

Later, while a languid nurse allegedly searched for the phone in nearby rooms, Lorraine asked, "What to do about Lily?"

"I told the Boss Lady! Where's that black bitch from, anyway?"

"Salmon Arm," said Annabel.

"How would you know?"

"I get around."

Sally snorted. "You believe everything you hear."

Lorraine, again, "What can we do?"

Silence.

"Let's take our diapers off! Do everything in our beds."

"*I'm* not a baby." Annabel stuck out her tongue at Sally.

"Don't fight. Please."

Melia came in, to finish them off. "That stolen folder makes a big trouble. Tomorrow Boss Lady seeing the *Big* Boss."

"Score!" cried Sally, and was first to grumble herself into a snore.

Next, Annabel.

Was Lorraine fainting? asleep? Warm dark flowed in the window. If only I could float out. That folder the Wanderer got—hers? *These are our stories.* I just have menus.

As June ended, a skunk sprayed the one car still in the parking lot.

CELEBRATING CANADA IN CARE

The hottest day yet.

In the dumpsters, smells ripened.

Not a weekday, hence no Activity, no doctors, no Lily.

Instead, nice Roberto, one of Angelique's nephews.

Offering walker-less Sally his arm, he steered her to the dining room, where she and Annabel joined a contingent able to anticipate the arrival, hours away, of a sheet cake with Dream Whip and Mexican strawberries atop. Holding maple-leaf flags, the roommates squabbled till the weak sweat of the old coated their flesh. Other residents sat, blank-eyed.

Alone, Lorraine tidied her menus. The italic font's rainbow colours pleased her, the dates one after another, the words poetically arranged.

golden macaroni &
carrot Confetti salad with
artisanal whole-wheat Bun
Macedoine of fruits
shortbread cookie with
selected Milks
and/ or tea/ coffee

Later, paging through water gardens, Lorraine heard a guitar. A bass led the distant gathering through *Au Clair de la Lune, Frere Jacques, Alouette*.

Angelique stopped by, to share berries dipped in chocolate. She came from yet another island and had twin boys.

The first time Mr. Chang waved hello, his chair had one flag taped to the control pad. Two, next time. Then clusters, on the push-bar. Beside him today trotted a hefty sixty-ish daughter and a Jack Russell. Smiling, Mr. Chang held the dog's leash.

The Rec Director also beamed in.

"Howzitgoin?"

"Fine." Lorraine did like *The Maple Leaf Forever*.

Whir whir whir.

"You stole my phone!"

The Wanderer held some blue envelopes. She folded one into a booklet, proffered this while pointing at herself.

"Give my phone back *now!*"

The big wrinkled face contorted as the Wanderer scrabbled in her fanny pack for keys, clapped them against the booklet. Her eyes pleaded.

Lorraine gave in. Considered this mime.

"How? There's always someone at the nurses' station."

The Wanderer pointed, jabbed towards Lorraine and at 17-A's other beds. Her mouth (no teeth) gaped in an unheard scream, closed, re-opened.

Lorraine considered further.

"We can try."

A scarf of violet silk passed from one woman to the other.

Alone again, Lorraine ran the silk through her fingers (thinner every day) while thinking of Lily's Alicia so far away. Of Lily's low wages, her minimal benefits and non-existent job security. Her tedious, often distasteful tasks. Her struggle to keep status among the staff. Her limited English. How her hair went limp as a shift ground on. How, at her touch, some white residents showed disgust. The river of silk ran over Lorraine. And the Boss Lady's life? No strength remained for that. She drowsed till Annabel scooted in, the advance guard before Roberto with Sally clutching his arm.

"Not enough fucking strawberries! Or flags. Not *fair*. My neck hurts."

"Wasn't that a cute guitar boy? Love to find him in my bed!" Annabel winked. "Eric went to a *real* Canada Day party, so he couldn't come today."

"Bullshit!"

Then supper came, and happy Sally's leftover cake read *Ca*, in pink.

Lorraine ignored her tray. "The Wanderer has an idea. We can help."

"She stole your phone!"

"To get our attention." Lorraine's voice stayed calm.

Annabel frowned. "How can she have an idea if she can't talk?"

"*Won't* talk, dummy. Teevee-gal *can't*. Don't you two want cake?"

"She wants to get back at—them." Lorraine gestured inclusively.

Annabel scraped cake onto Sally's plate. "Yes!"

"We must be ready. She can't predict when."

"When *what*? I don't like her. She threw—"

"Shut up!"

Lorraine closed her eyes. Annabel had the gist, and Sally'd need to hear it all again anyway.

DOING TIME

Sunday was hot. Zero Activity.

Monday, also hot, was a stat. Zero *Bingo,* zero doctors. The dumpsters grew rank. Gulls perched, swearing, on the closed lids. Julio, sent to Delivery to kill rats, did nothing but claimed the coyotes would eat them soon.

"Another lazy man," said Angelique.

Lily came back.

As she worked nearby, Lorraine closed her eyes against *rustle click push squirt wipe rub shove* but inhaled the aide's fragrance of tall dewy grass by the bus stop.

Lorraine's skin didn't fit. Her breath tasted bad. She napped.

For Annabel, Lily brought a hair clip and *Chatelaine*.

"Real silver!" The old shining head turned this way, that.

"Stupid! Remember how she tricked you?"

The aide said, "Your walker, Mrs. Knox. This time maintenance fix perfect." Strong hands massaged the resident's shoulders.

Lorraine, waking, found her dresser drawers rearranged

"See? More room for my menus!"

Sally snorted. "Lily just wants back in our good books."

"To atone," Annabel offered.

"How come *you* know that word?"

From 17-B gunshots reverberated, and shortly the Wanderer rolled into 17-A.

"Hello there!" Annabel waved *Chatelaine*.

Lorraine said, truthfully, "That's a nice dress you're wearing." The adaptive garment wasn't tucked in, though. A nude thigh, varicose, protruded.

"Such a bitch, Lily, letting you go out like that." Sally poked the fabric into place.

"Bitch," echoed Annabel.

Everyone smiled as the Wanderer handed over Lorraine's phone.

DOING MORE TIME

At Tuesday's *News & Views,* Annabel reported, people talked about Big Man biting an orderly. "We didn't even open the *Province*."

A doctor visited Lorraine.

After supper a bat landed on 17-A's windowsill.

Flapping towels, Annabel and Angelique rushed about till the creature swooped away.

"Close window."

"Stupid!" Sally cried. "By morning there's no air left."

"No oxygen," said Annabel.

"You studied chemistry?"

Angelique rolled her eyes.

Drinking water, Lorraine felt dry as drought.

Josie came by. "Little treat, girls!" Twinkies.

Sally ate them all, left the wrappers on her table and limped to the sink to splash hands and hot face.

"You've spilled, I'll skid!"

"Then skedaddle to your damn friends, Annabel." Sally grabbed paper towels.

"At least I *have* friends. And family, *Mrs.* Knox."

"Eric is a retard, Eric is a retard!"

"Fatty fatty two-by-four!"

Wads of wet towel flew, Lorraine sobbed, the Boss Lady entered.

"Quiet time, ladies?" She scanned the room. "Mrs. Knox, obesity shortens lives. Try to control yourself. That cellphone's back? No one told me."

After she left, a whiff of skunk remained in the air of 17-A.

WEDNESDAY

Midnight showers had suppressed the dumpsters' fermenting odour, but it rose again with the sun. The crows didn't attend *Crafts* to explore playdough's tactile pleasures, nor squeeze remotes with bleeding claws. They strutted about squawking while the rats and their babies snoozed in the warm dark rimmed with gold. Yearling gulls chased an eagle until, bored, it soared so its pursuers heeled away down the air.

Sally grumped, "Can't the bloody Wanderer get on with it?"

In the elevator, the Boss Lady lectured Annabel. The resident crossed her eyes.

Lorraine received from the Wanderer an Ambrosia apple and a photo of a willow-edged river curving away. At bedtime, a nurse checked her vitals. Her roommates didn't let their eyes meet.

THURSDAY, FLOWER-ARRANGING

Muggy. Rain forecast.

Lorraine lay on a gurney by 17-A's door, helpless before a doctor's order for a bedsore treatment over in the hospital.

Annabel stroked her roommate's hand.

Sally adjusted her walker. Too high. Too low.

"Fuck!" she shouted.

As if signalled, the TV in 17-B burst out *In the criminal justice system,* the volume rising to a bellow for *police, who investigate crime.* The Wanderer exited, holding a flag. Snapping it downward, she raced for the nurses' station.

Lily ran towards the roaring *These are their stories,* but Lorraine extended one arm off the gurney. She got the aide across the diaphragm.

Winded, Lily fell.

Sally threw herself upon her walker so it and she collapsed, then screamed.

Officer down! Teevee-gal laughed. Her rictus turned to hiccups as she handed the remote to Annabel. *Bang bang,* gunshots. *Two dead here.*

Annabel scooted to the linens while aides, LPNs, even a nurse responded to Sally's cries.

Lorraine sobbed. Her arm drooped from the gurney.

Just a kid, roared Jerry Orbach.

A black kid way out of his neighbourhood, Chris Noth sneered. *Of course he had to die.*

To the staff crowded into 17-B, Orbach blared *Where's justice?*

"Look, Teevee-gal's laughing!"

"Who knew she could?"

A shout, "You won't tell where it is, will you? You bad girl," laughing.

"Very bad!" Pats on the tattered fingertips.

In the hall, an LPN bent to Lorraine. The Boss Lady glanced their way but stalked on into 17-B, grasped the TV's cord, traced it to the outlet, pulled.

Silence.

"No one thought of that?"

Hiccups racked Teevee-gal.

"Or noticed this? You, attend to her. You, get rid of that TV. Shove it out the window for all I care. I'll page a doctor," gesturing at Lorraine. "The rest of you, back to work! No one's at the nurses' station."

Lily got to her feet.

There came the noise of a truck grinding into gear.

"Fucking great!" Sally shouted from across the hall. *"Did you hear me?"*

Obedience cleared the room.

Lorraine almost welcomed her pain, as suggesting a correctable mechanical wrong, and waited calmly for the analgesics to kick in, while hearing Sally's tale. Scrambled, yes—yet she and Annabel saw just how staff had huddled by jumbled human and metal limbs while the unseen Wanderer reached the window, her *whir-whir* inaudible under *Law and Order*.

Out flew the blue files, three, four, twelve, butterflies shedding hundreds of white inner wings as they tumbled. Twinkling paperclips, staples. Screech of plunging gulls. The truck heaved up the dumpster so its maw could vomit out all waste, everyone—but the Wanderer didn't stay to see that.

Sally finished telling just as the nurses' station broke into uproar.

"Score!" cried Annabel.

FRIDAY, BAKING

Overnight, the skunky vehicle stayed in the parking lot as the soft persistent summer rain of the West Coast began to fall. At dawn, animals drank. Birds stepped through puddles, shook rainbows off their wings.

With her trolley, Lily entered the watery light of 17-A. One woman had a bandaged ankle, one lay still, one clutched a jar of Sicilian olives.

The Boss Lady, clacking along, met and re-met Mr. Chang several times before she observed him waving at her.

"You want *what?*"

He asked again.

"A dog? To live here? D'you think I'm running a kennel?"

Such Language

FUCK YOU, THE MESSAGE TAPE SAID ONE OCTOBER DAY.

I pressed Replay. Yes, *Fuck you*, bracketed by *mmm* sounds. A high voice. Strained. Inside the *mmm*, were there words? Was the last one *Lauren?* After several replays I thought the terminal consonant wasn't *n*.

Today, if Henry and Jake and I were together as a family we'd all have cellphones. Even on a landline we'd each have a message box to accommodate a caller desiring to say to me, specifically, *Fuck you*. In 1985, however, I was living with an answering machine and an eleven-year-old son and a forty-three-year-old husband. I pressed Erase. At once this seemed a mistake, but then Henry and Jake arrived home from soccer, so it didn't.

Their news: a team would be chosen for league play. Our boy was hopeful. So was Curtis, his friend. After practice, as usual, they'd all gone to Tom & Jerry's, with Curtis's mum Melanie, for celebratory hot chocolate.

"The new TV there is huge," Henry reported.

"Don't get addicted to the screen, son," said Jake.

The answering machine's message indicator still showed a luminous red *3*. Before I could stop him, Henry listened. "Hang-ups. They're all grand-mère."

"My mother?"

"Madame?" Jake made the formal term affectionate.

"She puts the phone down hard. I can tell it's her."

Listening to the bangs, I saw my widowed mother at her desk. My father had built in a drawer for the phone directory, a well for pencils, and a bookshelf holding Churchill on WWII (six vols) and de Gaulle's *Mémoires de guerre* (three). The pages were soft-edged.

When Jake met my parents, he'd admired that desk. "Distinctive. A craftsman's work."

"Just a village carpenter." My self-deprecating father, very pleased.

Jake's praise also won over my mother, till then disconcerted by my choice. "Lauren, I expected you to marry an intellectual."

Now we said, "You're right, Henry."

How could we tell? Still I don't know.

Getting the machine was my idea, of course. Play, Replay, Erase, Rewind, Stop. Under the translucent cover, the brown plastic ribbon swelled and shrank in its orbits.

My mother asked Henry, "What is Lauren's new nonsense?"

They were piling her winter clothes into her freezer, because his science teacher said this would kill moths.

"It's me saying the greeting, grand-mère!"

She did "her wave thing," a backhand sweep to fend off unwanted data. "A telephone is not to prevent people from talking."

"Grand-mère, you can say whatever you like!"

"I am not a machine."

Then they went out to check the seedlings in her cold-frame, and, in the five months since, grand-mère had never left a message.

I began thawing dinner. "Don't turn it off, Henry."

"Let me guess, Lauren," said Jake. "You just want peace and quiet?"

I kissed him. We both hugged Henry.

Truth be told, we'd been grateful for the machine. Too often my mother phoned as we got home, or were eating, and she rarely began by asking about Henry's game, Jake's sweet peas. Never about my day at the library.

"Lauren, I have bought Seville oranges. It is the marmalade time."

"Lauren, the *Globe* is like you. It thinks the UN can save the world. Or have you still not read today's editorial?" (Her one-two punch.)

"The language I hear on the bus! That young people should speak so. Brutal, ugly. Such words my grandson must never say."

"North Americans are ignorant. They do not understand war." My mother grew up in Lyon, France. Twenty-nine in 1945 when history wrote *That's all folks,* she'd spent the war by her own mother's bed, a witness to one slow, agonizing death.

"Jake, what about my dimmer switch? And that play you did the sets for, the *Courier* review is not favourable."

Amiably he winked. "One-two!"

Now we could enjoy our meal, letting the phone ring. After dinner, Henry called her. Jake and she consulted about the stocks they prepared, the sourdough and brioche they baked.

But she'd call me later, too.

On book club nights, my head awhirl from *Down Among the Women* or *Revolutionary Road*, I was glad not to hear her voice. "To discuss fiction, what for? Imaginary people do things and do things, then it's over. From biography, memoir, one can learn."

At our last meeting we'd learned that Andrea, trying to conceive, during sex with her husband felt like Atwood's handmaid. Myrna was reporting a former therapist to the college of psychologists. Lesley took water from her kid's school swimming pool to a lab for analysis.

"Lauren, the woman who brings my newspaper *hurls* it at my door. Crash! Then in her car she speeds away."

My mother did not drive, *conduire*, so was ignorant of the machine's sweet solitude. Nor did she ever work outside the home. Nor, because of their war wounds, did she and my father fight. They met at a train station in Lyon where his unit wasn't supposed to be. The Liberation, some mix-up. He was short, dark, English. She was tallish and blonde.

"George was so well-spoken. In the war, people cursed very much. You can have no idea. *Foul* language. The English term is precise."

Sitting on a fourteenth-century stone wall, these two talked in their limited French and English of their favourites, Bacall and her Bogart. Under the stylish cynicism, such tenderness. The dialogue, so telling. They agreed that their own countries were done for. In that soil—soaked in filth, caustics, human blood—no good life could grow. They crossed an ocean, a continent. At home in Vancouver, we spoke English.

In kindergarten, my son Henry said, "Grand-mère, French is pretty." My mother had not approved of our placing him in French immersion ("So North American, pretending to be someone you are not"), but thereafter she spoke only that language to him.

Fuck you, that tape said.

Tape. Looking back, aging technophiles can feel like strangers. Were things so primitive in our own adulthood? Many patrons and a few library staff cried when we tossed the card catalogue. To avoid electronics, some librarians even retired. Not I. Laborious female typing, ribbons that oozed or faded—such waste.

Early answering-machine greetings assumed callers were deaf or slow-witted. *After the second beep, you have thirty seconds to talk.* Soon users got cute. Couples spoke in unison, cats mewed, toddlers whined. The CBC's contest for best greeting got hundreds of entries.

Henry thought the best excuse for not getting a message deserved a prize. *The tape broke! The machine got unplugged when I was vacuuming!* At this my book club laughed, confessed their lies. Rosalind's was *The cat stepped on the Erase button.*

"Actually true," she said later at our weekly lunch, eaten quickly as we were both work-addicted. "Would I lie to you?" Her angled smile. At club we teasingly called her Fair Rosalind.

Now, back from a book-evening, I could let my brain cool. Then, "Hello, mother. Can you talk for a bit now?"

"Why not? I'm alone, am I not?" Which took my mind off book club.

The club's discussion always started with the nuts and bolts.

Didn't he realize?

How could they keep up the pretense?

Where'd she think that would get her?

Too soon, my friends uncorked the wine and their own narratives. Same queries, more tears. Infidelity (Andrea's husband), ungrateful children, unprincipled colleagues, migraines (Robin), carpal tunnel and candida (Lesley), debt and renos (Myrna), Rosalind's fibroids, later her infertility, the stressful travel her job required in northern BC. I was the only one not in therapy. Nor did I refer to Jake as my partner, a new term then.

I'd have preferred to stay with the novels, whose codes drew me. Small things, details. Clothes. Metals. Weather paint birds food gestures light clocks stars floors water smells—such language told so much in *The Color Purple, Man Descending, A Jest of God*. At our satellite lunches, Rosalind and I often talked of imagery.

What story could I tell my friends?

Jake and I loved Henry like mad, all possible clichés. That love made two pillars that held the marriage firm, and between us our child swung happily. I loved my job, airports, deadlines, the intense management meetings till ten PM. My health was fine.

Jake's nickname was Mr. Sunshine, his temperament perfect for a set designer doing genuine work amid fat theatre egos. No, not love at first sight, he didn't read fiction, had an erratic income. Irrelevant. Over twelve years our interests hadn't converged, but almost daily we gladly found each other in the big bed. I couldn't believe how little sex Myrna Lesley Robin Andrea had. Of such poor quality, too. Rosalind, single, did better.

Was I just boring? Shallow? Once Robin spoke of Hallmark families.

Was I in denial? Andrea felt she'd denied for years her need for orgasm.

Certainly no one liked my remarking, "Anaïs Nin is so self-centred."

"But Lauren, we only have one life? We all just want to be happy?" Rosalind. Her rising tone to end a declarative sentence: another 80s symptom.

Again on the tape, *Blur fuck blur you blur.*

Replay. Erase.

The hang-ups also increased. *Bang. Bang.*

"Jake, what do you think we should do?"

"Ask Henry. He's on Madame's wavelength."

Indeed he was. Our son had his own room at her house, and sometimes they apologized for not speaking English to us.

"Let's not drag Henry down with adult stuff."

Jake shrugged. Again he was in between contracts. Maybe a *Private Lives?* Another theatre sought an angel for *Equus.* Waiting, he'd repaint our living room. Colour chips brightened the litter of sketched horses, wrought-iron balconies. Henry admired them all.

I did call my mother more often, but our talk jolted. In my ears still ran the music of my parents' conversation, fluent, inquiring.

Soon after Jake and I married, I applied for a new library job. The competition, tough. Also male—this still carried weight. Evenings, I polished my resume and my vision (another 80s word). Then too, Jake was between theatre jobs. He'd helped to re-roof Myrna's house, been an extra in a local TV series (Rosalind got him that), tree-planted near Terrace. Now he sulked.

"Jake, I have to finish typing this."

"Lauren, come to bed." That language we spoke fluently.

I got the job. I got pregnant. To baby Henry I talked about everything. Caring for him, Jake and I learned another common tongue. He took that same tree-planting contract for years. We always thought maybe I'd fly up to Terrace, a little getaway. Thus patterns form.

This autumn went on.

Both Henry and Curtis were on the league team.

My book club convened. *Home Truths*. Myrna raged at her husband's money messes. Robin analyzed her daughter's teacher's personality disorder. For once I too had a tale. At an IT conference, a catalogue specialist from Moncton made a pass at me.

"At least did you get drinks and dinner?" (Myrna.) "I can't believe you wouldn't take the opportunity!" (Rosalind.) "Not good-looking?" (Andrea.)

Once I went to soccer practice. Curtis's mum was lively, humorous, unlike tedious Lesley who was always on about loneliness. Melanie didn't read novels or use a computer, but we both disliked the coach and found Tom & Jerry's hot chocolate too sweet.

On a Tuesday, Henry noted ten hang-ups. Seventeen, Wednesday. That Friday the indicator said *30*. Only a few hurt our ears. Genuine messages were interspersed.

"A nuisance caller. I'll notify the phone company."

"Grand-mère," Henry insisted. "With some different bangs for disguise."

No patience remained in me after a day spent managing the sort of librarians who bring stereotypes to life. I called my mother. The old dial phone, how outrageously time-wasting! Two zeroes, a nine, three full rotations.

"You've called here twenty-three times."

"Hello, Lauren. How is Henry? How was your work today?"

Wozz. Her pronunciation was off. Wobbly.

"Mother, are you all right?"

She cried.

She also cried when at UBC I quit history for electronic languages.

My father reassured her. "Modern, precise. Like our Lauren."

During childhood evenings when I played and he did crosswords, my mother talked with him while skimming French periodicals. Even in English she was good at anagrams. Or she'd read aloud, translating as she went. These exchanges grew to full converse, allusions, flirty disagreements, laughter—until they remembered their witness to intimacy. Sent to bed, I'd read. That's how I started with novels. Because of their war, my parents slept badly. I'd wake, sensing vacancy in the big bedroom, and from the stairs hear that companionable murmur in the kitchen. In three decades they never ran out of things to say.

Grand-mère's gallbladder surgery was on Remembrance Day.

Always when I reached the hospital, the patient slept, Henry by her side with homework or a crossword. Later, I dropped him at soccer. Because of Tom & Jerry's, he and Jake weren't home till I'd had enough solitude to be sociable. All the machine's messages were real.

The rains began with *The Progress of Love*. Lesley's new therapist led her through rebirthing. Soon, weaning. Myrna's lover wanted to try bondage. Dared she? Everyone was supportive.

Andrea took a breath. "Lauren, we all open up. Why won't you?"

A planned intervention, I could tell.

"Acting so superior, holding back," said Lesley. Also, conceited.

Wilfully blind: Rosalind.

Emotionally unavailable, selfish, so left-brainy— Robin had resented me, apparently, "Forever! Time you got the message."

Such clichés. I went home raw. Another.

Nécrotique, my mother termed her gallbladder. "Henry can use that adjective at school." From her surgeon she'd got her stones, forty small grey polyhedrons. "For science class." She refused to recuperate with us, but minutes after we'd deposited her at home our phone rang.

"You may suffer this too, Lauren. At least there is a predisposition."

Troubling, how soon that call came.

Her recovery seemed slow. She, subdued.

Jake got her housecleaner to come more often, Henry took extra trips to library and video-shop, I blended her grocery shopping with ours. She accepted the changes. Did they make her sad?

Henry reported, "Grand-mère's scar was red like spaghetti. Now it's getting pink."

"Madame showed you?"

"I hope you didn't ask her?"

"She showed me in the hospital!"

"At least she stayed awake, for you."

Henry visibly decided to say, "Grand-mère wasn't asleep. She's scared to be a burden, like her own mother. She hurt for ages before she told you guys. I sat with her."

It came to me: if I went back to book club I could present her. *Mother-daughter stuff to share. Kind of heavy. When the child becomes the parent? You know?*

A most suitable issue. If.

Reassuringly, when *Private Lives* opened my mother did her wave thing.

"In the movie I have seen the best. Why spoil the memory?" Nor would she see *Equus*. "I have read this work. Kinky." This came out Frenchly, *quinqui*. "Unsuitable for Henry."

My book club went. Jake reported they'd bought him a drink afterwards, praised his set. Fuck those harpies. When Henry and I went, what impressed him was the animal. Jake's twisted aluminum strips only implied an airy shape, yet the tall creature was for sure a stallion, who bore his desperate rider powerfully.

So long ago.

Christmas approached. The Beta/VHS war was over; a new machine would gleam under our tree. I'd bought one for my mother too.

I asked her, "How is it, having your cleaner twice a week?"

"Certainly the house looks better."

Careful. "I meant, how do you feel about it?"

A blank look. No words. No one-two. *So much for open communication. I tried!* For my report at book club. If.

I drove home fretting, was still fretting when Jake and Henry arrived.

Our son threw his pack on the floor, shouted, "Why do we have to stay so long?"

"Son, you were glued to the TV."

"TV's *boring* there. I see Curtis every *day.*"

"Stop, Henry! I'm tired."

My parents, watching movies at home, got up to lower the volume if the characters shouted. To demand, to show anger—no, no, unless alone in my room. Grown up, I never swore in my mother's presence. Tried not to in Henry's. At work, such restraints don't apply. The Fiery Mouth of the Seventh Floor, that's me.

"Dad, *I'm* tired. Of him, of Melanie."

As with any complex problem, first comes meditation, often conscious, sometimes (as here) not. Certainty fills the dark mind then. Even if the solution looks peculiar, correctness shines. Clichés bounce up. *How could I be so slow? Why didn't I read the code?* Like other parents, Jake watched the practices. Like Melanie, lively and humorous on Mon Wed Thurs, plus weekends as league play moved on. A charming single mum. Sugary mugs, the boys absorbed. Not a reader. Not computer literate.

Jake and I soothed Henry. We ate, laughed, watched TV with him cosy in the middle.

After he slept, a quiet hour passed. *How long has this been going on? How could you?* Humiliating, unsayable clichés, dead idioms. Jake's toothbrush buzzed.

"Goodnight," I said. "I'm watching the news."

Then a PBS doc, the US invading Grenada. I dragged upstairs. At the sight of him in our bed, I U-turned to huddle by the TV till dawn.

Off Henry went to school, my clever boy. Then he'd go to grand-mère's, to make mince tarts. Her pastry, inimitable.

Mr. Sunshine was prone in the living room, applying tape by the baseboards to keep the floor clear of paint. He held the roll between his teeth.

"How long have you been fucking Melanie?"

Jake didn't tear the tape. Silence. Like greetings that give the avid caller only a circling whisper for unendurable seconds. *Hi there! Hal and Michelle are having too much fun to answer the phone, so leave a message.*

"It's got nothing to do with us. *Totally* separate, totally." Another 80s word.

Then why pray tell have you kept it secret?

"There's no difference for you and me! We make it nearly every day."

There is so. You have lied, in your body.

Mr. Sunshine scrambled up, headed for the door.

"Don't you run away! I'll call her. That'll be different!" The soccer list, by the phone. I dialled. *Fuck you* I'd say. Jake grabbed at the receiver. Ringing. I spat in his face, cliché. He backed off. *Thanks for calling. Melanie and Curtis aren't able. . .* A warm voice. Why wasn't she there, the bitch?

"You god-damned bastard. It's over."

I went to work.

Subsequently I repeated the above many tedious times. It's also possible to cry so often it gets boring. *Not tears again!*

"This isn't fucking necessary, Lauren!"

"Fucking her wasn't necessary!"

We could shout because our boy was helping to move grand-mère's sofa so her cleaner could vacuum behind. Then they'd watch *Charlotte's Web*. For hot chocolate they grated bittersweet, melted it over hot water. Neither admired Debbie Reynolds as the spider's voice. They were re-reading the novel. Soon they'd move on to Jimmy Stewart and Alastair Sim.

Henry would go on living in his home, Jake and I decided. We'd take fortnightly turns with him. How to tell them?

"Madame will think it's crazy." Here we agreed.

Shortly before Christmas, again the taped *Fuck you*, the muffled start and finish.

A woman. Myrna, Rosalind, Lesley, Robin, Andrea?

When I knew they'd be out I phoned, listening three times to spiteful Andrea who'd once asked Rosalind, "What do you want a baby for? You haven't even got a man of your own."

No match. Erase.

As I was driving my mother to our house on Christmas Eve she remarked, "You look worried, Lauren."

"I am." Which I hadn't planned to say.

"Is it Henry?"

"Is what? Has he said something?"

The car moved along the silent road. Snow in Vancouver isn't common. The whiteness brings a quiet that's always surprising. *She doesn't even answer me*, I could say at book club.

In January I escorted my mother to a game. She sat in the car with the heater on, to watch her grandson's team win. Melanie and Curtis were visible. Jake did not join us. No one went to Tom & Jerry's.

Next day, listening to the messages, my brain was full of a library crisis. Perhaps that freed my ears?

She'd had to struggle past the expletive's initial consonant. *He's fffucking you over.* As if in a movie my mother sat at her desk, her linen handkerchief wrapped round the receiver.

When at the next book club I opened her dossier of old age and frailty, when I observed how those greedy ears yearned for more, I knew the novelist's power. I *had* those women. Elated, I took them to wartime France to see my mother's loving guilt. They clasped their hands, wept softly. "Oh, Lauren, your poor mum. So hard, so sad." Next I catalogued her doctor's assessment, the geriatric social worker's, her housecleaner's. My husband's. Saying *Jake* axed open my throat.

"He, he, he's," horrible guttural, "been unfaithful. You can't imagine how long it's been going on."

"Years!" cried Fair Rosalind, and slid off her chair in a faint.

Later she said a hundred times, "Jake swore he'd told you."

"You knew, Lauren!" he himself shouted. "You couldn't believe I was just tree-planting in Terrace every year!"

Unread codes.

Done for. No good life could grow there again.

"I won't do that," Henry said. "I'm going to live with grand-mère."

"Mum and I will take turns, here." Jake spoke gently, though an hour earlier he'd been roaring, "Rosalind *talked* to me. For you I was just a dumb hunk." Those clichés too.

"I don't want *turns*," said Henry.

We tried.

We tried with my mother. She did her wave thing.

Not the weekends but the long turns were the worst.

Each summer Henry was with me for a month. Thirty-one days. Not long. Long enough to feel the child in his room close by in the apartment, to hear him breathe and stir in our shared air, to watch him dream, yet soon so soon to feel time draining and sucking away as it does during the speed-of-light week before the deadline set for the worst thing ever: helping my boy pack his little clothes, his books and games, and releasing him to the other parent.

Men have abounded, mostly sexual amateurs. An unsuccessful migrant word, that, its meaning muddled en route to a new tongue.

I still love my work. Friends, books, movies. Not plays. My son doesn't speak of his father.

Renaissance, that's what happened to grand-mère after Henry moved in. She died in her nineties, weeks after dancing at her grandson's wedding. What price did she pay for breaking her own code to send that foul message to her distant child? Not quite idiomatic. Crucial. She'd have wiped her lips, after. As for the answering machine, only last week I saw one at Too Much Collectables, in a window full of retro tchotchkes and faux-distressed chairs. I walked on towards Bean a While. Their coffee's good. Rosalind and I still meet sometimes, to talk. Lesley bought our machine. In itself that old technology was reliable.

Addresses

THE *RIGHT* APARTMENT. MEANING WHAT?

For Julie, that Jeremy be in it.

He did the hunting. Often she came along, still happy though sickish-dazed from The Pill.

Distinctive 1 BR suite even had a pantry. They moved in.

By then Julie could, just, see around him.

Also she knew she had never filled Jeremy's vision.

Sort-of arguments began, about The Pill. He, after research that took a lot of time away from his work, decided on condoms and foam.

In the distinctive building's entry, ceramic tiles formed octagons in a complex black-and-white arrangement. Stained glass. No elevator, no laundry room. The brass doorplates and fir floors were original.

"I checked." Satisfied, Jeremy closed the pantry door to work for hours so they could get ahead.

The paned windows stood tall, Julie not. They and the floors gleamed (she made sure of that), yet the elegant life once lived in these turn-of-the-century Vancouver rooms did not seem like anything she could match.

"What about a baby?"

"No, not yet. "

"When?"

"Not yet!"

Every time, Julie did not start a third interchange. Did she lack character? She did hunger for concord. They settled, kind of, on *soon*.

To be alone so much was still surprising. The magazines suggested picking one room each day, in rotation, for special cleaning. Julie did that. She ordered dress patterns, clipped recipes. Dinner was quite good sometimes. When Jeremy stayed late at the law office, she'd get into bed to wait, wanting him.

The spermicidal foam oozed all over the bed linen. Back and forth Julie walked to the laundromat, never meeting the same people there.

"You're pregnant?"

Jeremy couldn't or wouldn't believe she hadn't tricked him.

"Got your way, again." He slapped at the want ads, some red-circled. "I have no time for this. Can you at least follow up?"

Did *again* mean he hadn't wanted to marry?

Julie followed up, went further.

Of the place she found, he said, "It'll do for the time being."

What could time do but be?

Jeremy conceded the value of *2 BR nr shops, bus, beach,* although old frame houses with lacy trim had been bulldozed to make space for the *mod apt tower.* He deplored and Julie smiled at the lobby's earnest mural of a tropical sunset, the palm trees etched on the mirror by the mailboxes.

Of *1 prkg* he said, "Too bad you were careless. No money for that now."

Their own decor did please him. All paint and textiles and floor coverings were bone. Not the red lumps that dogs gnaw on, Julie knew that. White trim.

"Perfect neutrals. You do see how they don't call attention to themselves?"

The look of their Danish coffee table by the picture window also pleased Jeremy, for the north-east light enhanced the teak's grain. He removed their white cups to the kitchen as soon as they were empty.

"If only we were higher up." He opened his briefcase. *Under new mgmt.*

"That's you!" Silently Julie teased the hidden kicking child. "You get the second BR." Jeremy's desk, electric typewriter, file cabinet lived in the master.

The elevator too was soundless. Eyes closed, Julie couldn't tell whether the movement was up or down. The little tale she made of this uncertainty failed to amuse her husband after his stressful day in court.

"Do you mean that?" Jeremy asked.

He asked the question again when the baby's crying made Julie worry about the neighbours. "This building's solid concrete. I guess construction is another thing you just can't understand?"

Still Julie couldn't forget his pallor after the delivery, his joyful tears as he phoned long-distance to tell his parents and hers about James, while she trembled after a labour not much like that in the natural childbirth book.

Nor did she forget how they two began, at her *sunny Kits bach gt view.* Unusually for a girl, she'd had her own apartment. Jeremy had been surprised.

As Julie walked home from her little job in the weeks before their wedding, the pavement went all wavery rivery till she sped like a hydrofoil to the soaring elevator, the hall, her own door, and the engulfing heat of Jeremy's body. She'd been the initiator. He, taken aback. Shocked? Julie, though her mother and all the books warned against premarital activity, knew no doubt.

What was that view, anyway? The only one of her class to leave Victoria after secretarial school, she was just proud to have her own address.

Perhaps the sex was why the ceremony didn't change her?

After their honeymoon at Expo 67, the Kitsilano place felt cramped, wrong. Not even a nook for Jeremy's work.

He found, first, the *stately spacious 1 BR* at a good address, a fine old Dunbar mansion chopped into suites. Tall graceful trees darkened the place. Leaking radiators, mice. Julie and Jeremy shivered till he located the *distinctive* building.

"Where we'd still be, if you hadn't been careless."

She didn't remember much about Expo either. The hotel room. Fireworks, sugar, glitter, crowds. French actually spoken.

Now this high-rise.

The developer had built three towers close together, so Jeremy and Julie's living room in The Buckingham observed one in The Kensington where sofa, stereo, TV, and coffee table were similarly configured. The occupants were two men. Older, Julie thought, early forties.

The man with curly hair sometimes waved at the baby. Julie would raise James's tiny hand, smile. The overweight man didn't wave. If he noticed her across the airy gap he snapped the Venetians shut, even in sunshine.

Jeremy did the same. "I'm not paying rent to watch a couple of queers day in day out. We need our own house."

More things Julie hadn't understood.

James filled her hours. His certainty amazed her. *Now!* He cried with his mouth so wide his throat made a quivering red tunnel.

The neighbours Julie encountered in the elevator and by the mailbox were mostly retirees with little dogs, or young singles. Once just heading out of the lobby was a bald man in crisp shirt and shorts who held a placard, *Out of Vietnam Now!* Wasn't that an American war? He strode away. Was he old? Seeking other mums, she pushed James's stroller along the concrete walkway by Sunset Beach.

At the inadequate corner grocery she met the queers. Sam held back at first while Curly warned her never to buy the ground beef, but soon all three were picking through the faded vegetables together. Walking back, they smiled at the towers' palatial names.

One morning in The Buckingham's laundry room, Julie was giving James his bottle while waiting for the dryer to finish.

An old woman came in and smiled at the baby. "It is my lucky day! Mostly the people here have these foolish dogs. But you do not breast-feed? Is best."

Julie explained the theory of parents sharing equally in baby care. Under-thoughts about Jeremy rushed counter to her words.

In her tailored maroon dress, Mrs. Schatz moved about briskly, high heels clicking. Her wrinkles broke into new webs when she looked at James.

"So, how you like it here?" she asked. "What floor?"

The Schatzes lived on the view side of the eleventh.

"We will drink coffee. My husband will enjoy to see James. Also I invite Mr. Alexander, on the sixth. He appreciates art."

Before that happened, Julie met Sam and Curly again. This was at Sunset Beach, in the pause when the bridge's lamps begin to reflect on the greying water yet daylight still hovers over False Creek, stippling the waves pink or apricot.

Under a fine rain they ambled talking along the pebbled sands. James, held in his Snugli against Julie's warmth, kept tilting his head back to get the drops on his face. He smiled. So did Curly and Sam and Julie.

"How did you meet?" she asked as they left the beach. The bridge lamps were now shedding gold circles on the salty darkness.

The men exchanged looks and snickered, snapping the Venetians down. Both spoke. At last Curly managed, "We'd both been around enough to know what we wanted. We were ready."

As Julie with James rode up in the air she thought how the magazines said things just like that about deciding in the right way to get married.

"Where've you been? You're soaked. No umbrella again?"

She described their pleasant walk.

Jeremy made a face. "Queers are useless. That's why I don't like them."

"Is a tax accountant useless?"

"Who does Fatty work for? Other queers? And what does Pretty Boy do?'

Julie quit, though in fact Curly was the numbers guy and Sam the waiter.

"We need to get out. This isn't what I had in mind." He shoved a newspaper at her and stood waiting by the door into the master.

After skimming *Houses* Julie studied *Furnished Suites*. Some buildings said *Small child accepted*. What size might that be? How could she pay? She perused *Board & Room*. Water dripped off her hair on to the baby's smile.

"Nothing today."

The door closed. Shut out.

Now Julie did feel changed, though she still waited greedily for Jeremy to come to bed. Sometimes he slept on the sofa.

Time went on being.

James grew bigger, bigger. With pain he acquired teeth. He looked about, inquiring. He shook and pulled at his playpen's bars. Visiting the eleventh floor, he demonstrated how he would crawl soon.

Mr. Schatz chuckled. "He reminds me."

Julie silently ached to ask *Of whom?*

"Today Mr. Alexander is tired. He fights cancer," his wife sighed. She pointed at the tiny poppyseed pastries veiled in powdered sugar. "His favourites." For James she had baked rusks.

"He also is exile by a war," said her husband.

From the Schatzes' windows, the distant Olympic Mountains shimmered aquamarine. The stereo was playing classical. Nearer, Mount Baker shone like pearl. Victoria was clouded in drifts of white, invisible.

On leaving, Julie felt revulsion at the prospect of entering the apartment where she lived. She pressed James's thumb on L for Lobby.

By the mailboxes stood the bald man. He held a map.

"An impossible city," he said. "Vancouver's a simple place, the mountains are always north. Even New York's mostly a grid."

He was Julie's age. So thin in his sharply pressed Bermudas, paler even than bone. The map showed London, England.

"Are you going there?"

"Paris too. New York on the way back, if I'm not arrested." He tucked the map into a travel agent's folder. "See the galleries one more time."

"Are you Mr. Alexander?"

"Gary."

"Julie. This is James."

"Dear Mrs. Schatz," he said, "always wanting to feed me. Their sadness is unbearable, but I'll see them before I go."

"I hope you have a good time." What else could be said?

"Thank you." He inspected the baby. "Such sharp teeth! A little animal. So Julie, where are you off to?"

After a moment she said, "I have no idea."

Gary's eyebrows went up. "Better get one! Up and down, to and fro, then suddenly it's all over."

They shook hands warmly.

Soon after this, Jeremy began again about the oral contraceptive.

"You have to. We can't risk it. I insist."

Three things just like that with no breath between.

"You know it makes me sick." In disbelief she heard the shaking voice.

"Then I won't have sex with you."

After that there was only the morning dialogue before he departed for office or court.

"Will you?"

"No." Again, again. "*No.*" Julie gripped James so he howled and shoved his head into her armpit.

In the mirror, her lipstick looked wrong for the face she had now.

She still longed for sex with that changed man. Or had the persons called *Julie & Jeremy* not ever recognized each other? Had two others used their names to get married? She winced.

Daily his mother pushed James for hours through the West End to see the lines of bright windows in high-rises, low-rises, and to imagine their views. The Buckingham, later, seemed like nowhere she'd visited before.

Gary had reached London now, to stand alert in front of paintings. On the postcard he sent, a stern man wore olive and brown. Why was he painted? She did not show the card to Jeremy.

Mrs. Schatz said, "That is Bacon."

James stayed with her once while Julie went out to walk alone, a novelty. Along Denman and Davie she examined closely what was on offer in each store window.

On her return the child's lips were red with happy jam. "Must he go?" asked Mr. Schatz. Julie didn't tell that either.

Every day she and Jeremy did the dialogue.

Every day she feared saying, "All right, I'll do it."

And his loud voice shook. "I'm never having sex with you." Was the assertion wearing thin? Fear grew. She tried to imagine telling this. Who could hear? Mum, unthinkable. Her high school friends in Victoria knew nothing, were only engaged. In that too she'd led the way.

One morning Julie was so terrified that she pulled a dress over her head and gathered up James and went barefoot down to the beach.

The tide was ebbing; the water went west in a silver rush. The baby she held strove to move freely. Every pebble had a different shape. They hurt her feet. Why had she got married? When would Gary die? A dog chased sticks, plunged in and out of the water, shook rainbows. Julie waded. Cold first, then refreshing. She held James so his toes dangled in the waves. He kicked, chuckled. A long time went by, a short time.

Back at the palace, Julie pressed B and prayed.

She was folding her husband's socks.

"How is Mr. Beautiful?" Mrs. Schatz inspected Julie. "Rose is a good colour for you. Also it is a shade never out of style. But you do not wear shoes today?"

"In a hurry." Julie couldn't articulate.

"To leave. I see." Mrs. Schatz's manicured fingers stroked James's hair, tenderly. "Sometimes is best."

Julie carried the wicker laundry-basket out to the elevator.

"Thank you, my dear. You know where to find me."
Today her smart outfit was in navy. Every curl lay in place.
How could she and Gary look so neat?

Julie whispered, "I do."

"Be careful," said Mrs. Schatz, and disappeared.

Jeremy had gone to his work.

James banged and grumbled in his pen while Julie did hers.
With Dutch Cleanser on a toothbrush she toured the base
of the toilet. At the sink, her Q-tip winkled out guerilla dirt-
specks crouching where faucet met porcelain. She emptied the
medicine cabinet, washed each glass shelf. A hand took up a
remnant disk of The Pill. Seven/pink, twenty-one/blue, each
pellet snug in its cell. Then the other hand held a glass of water.

"Can't risk it," she told James, who screamed from
behind his bars. "We must be careful."

Soon Julie visited her doctor. Graciously he renewed
her prescription but gave her a critical look.

Jeremy asked later, "Can't you even button your blouse
right?"

The card Mr. Alexander sent the Schatzes from Paris
showed a sculpture of a pregnant goat. She looked lustful
and witty.

Mrs. Schatz said, "He says he will go home very soon.
His lady-friend from before has a place in Ithaca, New
York. He can be ill there."

War, love, art, cancer. How did someone her age get
such a history?

Though swallowing eagerly, Julie still defied her
husband. His daily shouts seemed an omen of rape. Were
they both crazy? She had no answers, only a baby.

In James's room stood a chaise longue for night feedings. Julie now slept there. Once crying woke her, but James was asleep, her own cheeks dry. Another time, getting up to pee, she saw Jeremy prone on the sofa. Their own double bed was smooth, its pillows plump. None of this could appear in any magazine.

Julie took James to visit her old workplace.

Wanting to look well, she wore her rose dress. Its length was out of style, she saw on reaching the office.

Julie told various lies while she and the girls had their happy time catching up in the coffee-room, the table a cosy dither of cookies and doughnuts and James's applesauce. Julie's replacement was friendly. They giggled together over the manager's limited Dictaphone skills.

He himself was amiable, tickling her boy under the chin. "You got a really important job here, Julie!"

Then the girls must get back to work.

The bus stop was across the road that once led to *sunny Kits bach*. Headache. Exhaustion. No umbrella. The bus was slow to arrive, slow crossing the bridge. James squalled and flailed as they neared The Buckingham, not the right place, Julie knew that at least, though in the downpour she couldn't find her keys, scrabbled in her purse again, couldn't, was spiralling into a tizzy when Sam and Curly appeared.

"Come up to our place."

The Kensington's murals showed Mediterranean waters of a sultry indigo not possible to imagine in English Bay.

"What's in The Windsor's lobby, I wonder?"

"We got in, to look. South-west," Curly answered. "Reds, pinks."

"Your elevator's quiet too," Julie remarked.

"Yes. Hard to tell if it's up or down."

As they started along the hall, Sam gestured towards their door but stopped himself. "Of course you know your way, Julie!"

When he took off his hooded rain-jacket, on one temple was revealed a large bruise. Julie didn't ask. He pointed. "You'd think they'd attack Curly, he's so cute, but more often it's me. Because I've got him, I guess."

After his bottle, James slept among the sofa cushions. Julie found her keys. Curly brought coffee, shoving comics and beer cans away to make room for the tray. Sam smoked. Julie inhaled her first cigarette since meeting Jeremy.

In their bathroom were far more bottles tubes jars than she and he owned. His contempt twanged in her ear. On the door hung two silky robes. Emerging, she managed a glance into the bedroom. The mattress was bare, with fresh folded linen stacked ready.

"We'd like to paint it purple," Sam said, "but when we go we'd just have to do that boring beige again."

"Go where?"

"We're planning to buy a house."

Curly chuckled. "To be as purple as we like." He touched Sam's head.

Back in the living room, Julie collected her essentials. How strange, to look out from here towards her present address. Not that there was much to see. In a lower suite, a coffee table displayed a big platter, elliptical and brightly glazed. It drew her eye.

In The Buckingham's lobby stood Mrs. Schatz, dressed for lunching out. That morning the expected news had arrived from Ithaca. Also the Schatzes had decided to get a little dog, to care for.

One Two Three Two One

"WHY GET SO WORKED UP, ELLEN?" My mother often asked that.

Also, "Why don't you just find someone and move out?"

And, "Why should you get special treatment?"

My father said, "Don't slouch dear, you're too pretty," or, "Don't sigh so," or, "Those maraschinos are for my old-fashioneds."

"Ellen, leave his cherries alone."

Standing in their kitchen by their huge fridge, I was twenty-nine. Thirty was clearly in view, other things not. While my Dad spoke on and on, I considered old-fashion*ed*. Whip cream. Log trucks. Fly zone.

"So sweetie," he finished, "buy your own."

"Really, you two," my mother said. "How you do go on."

I didn't see any *two*, but this isn't the kind of story that describes ad nauseam the characters' feelings, so no more on that. Events only. *An* old-fashioned. Noun omitted, adjective solo. Then such isolated linguistic phenomena interested me, discrete, unlinked by storyline.

My mother wrapped up her presentation. "You make me tired."

Later I carried home from the grocery a jar of maraschinos so large it'd need subdividing to fit into my bar fridge.

By the sidewalk a man on hands and knees examined a stone on the grassy verge. Gently he touched a curl of grey lichen, smiled up at me. Lawrence Whatsit. We'd gone to the same high school, he a year ahead. Didn't the Whatsits live nearby? And wasn't his mother dead? Lucky Lawrence. He laughed at the cherries. We ate, sitting on the grass, and licked our sticky fingers and laughed. The lichen frilled up like egg white on a frying pan. (That's the first simile, of very few.)

"Touch," Lawrence invited. The lichen: a delicate leather. (Also few metaphors.) I smelled it, looked through his magnifying glass while he explained, but this isn't one of those stories puffed out with data about parrots or antique clocks or saffron, so no more. What happened, the doings that took me every- and nowhere—in this story that's all I intend.

Lawrence concluded, "Lichens rule the world."

Then he had to go, for his mother was expecting him. It was the father who'd died. Wishful thinking.

Translation awaited me, so I went home to the top floor of my parents' house, one enormous attic room. Why live there? Private entrance 800 sq ft, FP, HW floors, alcoves, dormers, claw-footed tub. . . Mostly, to annoy my mother.

Outside, the wind sang in the trees (personification). As a child I'd dreamed of floating out and over those maples, far away. (Not emotion. Fact.) I had a hot plate and used it, but fiction garnished with recipes doesn't appeal to me.

My parents' TV and bathroom and furniture were all bigger than mine, their magazines glossier, so from time to time I regressed to the lower floors. My father and I would converse.

"YY?" he'd say.

"XXX."

"No, YY! And also YYYYY!" he'd retort.

I'd shout back, "XXX, and XXIV for that matter!"

"What?" He was growing deaf. Shorter, too, with age.

My mother did the ending. "Oh let up, you two! Such a to-do."

Our family dialogues could have featured as idiom samples for ESL students. Let up. Really. How you do. Worked up. To-do.

For a translator, idiom offers the most brilliant challenges. (Except poetry. I have not got that far.) Back then I translated botanical articles, conference proceedings, minutes, reports. (Even in such meagre soil, metaphor sprouts). Idiom drew me, still does, a private tongue parenthetical within a given language. Parasitical? No. Idiom enlivens, does not destroy the host.

Like lichens, I told Lawrence, languages rule the world. Nor are they separate, especially those spoken by millions—Mandarin, English, Spanish. Oh, at the centre, where the standard flies, they're distinct, but at the margins the rules get bitten to bits (repetition, alliteration), and people speak amazing hodgepodges. There's far more margin than centre. Look at any page. See how metaphor slides in? All this and much more I said to Lawrence, but as backdrop that'll do. No elaborate analogies between Chinook and the symbiosis of algae or fungi and love. In too many stories, such comparisons drag the doings off course.

At the Whatsits' house, Lawrence's territory was the basement suite. High, south-facing, sun-washed. Small animals jarred in alcohol stood in ranks on his shelves. Skins, skulls. A globe for twirling. A cupboard door that must stay closed till spring because a spider's egg-mass clung to the hinge. I wouldn't have cared.

When Lawrence and I came upstairs after a morning on his bed, his mother was ready for us with waffles, peaches, crème fraîche.

"I remember you, Ellen," smiling. Some high school event, awards for science students.

After eating, Lawrence took us back downstairs, only in part to make love again. "She pushes in too close," he frowned. "Keep your guard up." Too close? Such a thing, in a mother!

Familiar, peculiar, other, darling, such was Lawrence. Botanical Latin was only one shared idiom. Others: our bodies, devotion to work, facing a fourth decade in houses where we'd always lived. Bonded like lichen to stones we were, another simile, my guard down.

Lichens. Lawrence photographed them. For drug companies he analyzed their properties. For universities he identified them. He lectured.

"I'm portable," he said. "So are you." He set his globe twirling. "Languages and lichens are everywhere."

To detach, dislodge, float like bursting clouds of spores (another) was our hypothesis. To live nowhere seemed a fine plan. Our preparations for marriage were simple. We saw a travel agent, got new laptops, and at his mother's urging rented a post office box.

My father told me, "I like him, dear, but that's no way to live."

"Why such a fuss? We'll have the house to ourselves."

"What did you say?"

My mother had spoken with perfect clarity.

For nine months Lawrence and I travelled. On airstreams of desire and thermals of spontaneity we floated about Europe, Asia. The green algal cells in the symbiosis, were they him? Or me? Who made the colourless fungal strands? See how metaphor bloats up to excess?

His mother wrote when the eggs hatched. She'd carried hundreds of spiderlings out to the sunshine. Although I wouldn't have bothered, to me her act showed reliability.

Lawrence frowned. "She's overdoing it."

I translated. Globally I faxed and emailed, loving how Lawrence and I and our work diffused ourselves electronically. Dispersal. Possibly even then I loved that as much as him.

For my birthday, the mother-in-law sent a pretty book with blank pages. "Thought you might jot down your doings."

Such a thing, never owned, never done. (Don't worry, no quotes.) To note, scribble—exotic, for a rigorous translator of proceedings.

My own mother had recently shrunk, but now her letter blew her up again. "Your father and I think of renting out the attic. Waste of space."

"He'd never do that!" Lawrence hugged me. "Your Dad loves you, Ellen. Don't worry, my sweetheart."

Hug hug.

For my father, Lawrence photographed the two of us. He shot lichens—crustose, foliose, fruticose—*enough*. Events *only*. He wrote, lectured. In Turkey and Malaysia he made good contacts. In bliss we lived. No one, not even she, can take that time away.

When I began to vomit each morning, Lawrence stayed happy. (It is possible, given later doings, that he grew even happier.)

My whole body hurt. Respiration, digestion, excretion, translation, circulation all malfunctioned. Only reproduction hummed along. After an Athenian doctor opined that a difficult pregnancy was best endured "at home," back we went, at Lawrence's insistence, to our sole country Canada, and our lovely airport living ceased.

Mrs. Whatsit crouched in her familiar house.

After the vomiting came faints and vicious headaches, and in their train eclampsia. She never failed to soothe and feed. We stayed upstairs with her so she could help quickly, though Lawrence longed for a space of our own.

From my own mother came no word about Fussing or Worked up. She met my tear-bleared gaze. "Terrible, isn't it? Now you know."

Lawrence published. He consulted. Everywhere lay slides of lichens—cloud-grey, celadon, duck's egg. My translations slept unattended like Snow White. I did not care. No prince would come.

Mrs. Whatsit read aloud from baby books. Chuckling, she told of her son's infancy.

"Can't you see Ellen's tired?" Lawrence's anger meant protection, but I closed my ears to him, admitted only that soft female voice.

After many hours of labour they got it out of me. An army had trampled through my body (this one extended metaphor I permit, pleading extenuating circumstances) and then stomped off across obliterated borders. The occupation over, defeat at first felt unimportant. That no one was inside sufficed, that no one any longer lived off the country of me. I can still close off the metaphor, am not so far gone as poetry. The scale in the delivery room told seven pounds. I'd have believed seventy.

We moved downstairs, into the sunny basement suite.

The baby wouldn't take the bottle. Mrs. Whatsit became agitated.

"Why fuss?" asked my mother. "She'll give in. It's the rule."

A pattern of feeds and sleeps developed, Lawrence's mother claimed. Simultaneously, metaphors I'd played with on pages set aside in the journal leaped up. They morphed into narratives. The paper absorbed ink as mosses do rain (third simile).

Now what were we going to do?

Lawrence and I, from fifteen to approximately thirty, had been *acquainted*. When we *really met* (there's a translator's test!), *we fell in love*. We married. We were *happy,* easy in every tongue. He now looked much older than when we ate cherries on the grass.

Me too. My father said, "You were so pretty, dear, such a pity."

Back to translating. Compared to the brutal tasks impressed by pregnancy, the glide/slide from language to language was easy. My work done and invoiced, I bought a separate notebook and left behind first person. Yes, I abandoned her, pushing off into the singing trees of third, dozens of thirds. Metaphors, similes were the least of the hijinks I got up to.

I had to come down when Lawrence and I rented our own apartment. After I'd finished my daily stint of translation and wanted to write, I'd leave her in the building's laundry room (why would anyone take a baby?) to enjoy the dryer's vibration, or put her out on the balcony to feel the spinning rain. The trees were way down, much too far to float, but Lawrence's mother fussed. She got worked up. She came over ever more often to *help*. (Such a test, that common verb!) To escape her, Lawrence spent hours back in his old room with the dead drunk moles. She was here, he was there, I was nowhere I knew.

Next we tried my old attic.

Renovation easily created a baby-area and one for Lawrence's work, but that space had all been mine. Since my teens, my parents had hardly entered. To cram in with a man, a baby, Mrs. Whatsit more often than not, and to sense underfoot, literally, my own parents—intolerable. (Also my mother's word for Mrs. Whatsit.)

My father often clumped upstairs. He liked Lawrence. He bought a TV series on fungi narrated by a potato-in-the-mouth Brit and cuddled the baby while watching my old screen, still there, still small. Dad turned the volume up and up.

Defeated, Lawrence agreed to move back to his mother's house.

Her bedroom was next to the baby's. "So convenient!" she said, delighted. "So easy to get up with her at night!"

I agreed. While I translated, Mrs. Whatsit brought coffee, baked snacks, took phone calls, ran errands. All these Lawrence had long ago cut her off from doing for him.

My narratives were now my real work. I hid the notebooks. My mother-in-law didn't need to see the massy life swelling from her gift. Things were bad enough already. In the guest room, Lawrence couldn't get it up. He tried to lure me to the golden basement, apparently not understanding the words I spoke about this. A long time went by before he grasped that no sex was possible unless conception was 100% impossible.

After the extraction I'd asked for a tubal, but the docs hedged and huffed. So it was up to him. So he requested a vasectomy, and got zero medical huffing. We made love once. Made. Hard work. Then I got all worked up. Until my period, no narratives came.

"Ellen, once a month is not enough."

What standard of language was this? This rule was never before ours, not mine now. Near the Whatsit house was a park. Sitting near windy trees, I wrote narrative. At night I translated. Thus, very busy.

Quite a good time, that.

Lawrence and I and she went for dinner to my parents' house.

My father: "You're too thin dear. Slouching makes you look thinner."

My mother: "Don't fuss. Can't you see she's having trouble?" She fetched his jar of maraschinos. "Here, Ellen, eat."

"What?" my father asked. "What is Ellen having?"

The baby cried.

Because Lawrence's mother was not there to soothe her, he took her up to my attic and walked about. His steps, her cries resounded above. I watched TV with my parents. Stuck in those big fat armchairs, they looked littler all the time.

Lawrence insisted I go back to the doctors. "You have to stop crying."

After my tubal, things changed yet were not better. Not *really*. Try that, translators!

A form letter came. Our post-office box was up for renewal. Mail had scarcely ever reached us thus, but we remembered the happy rental. We cried. Side by side, Lawrence and I turned and folded and smoothed that shoddy official paper till it became soft as muslin. For days that form lay on the dresser in the guest room. One of us would pick it up, read, smile, cry.

He announced, "This is despair."

His saying so was pivotal to the plot. A hundred times I'd felt myself alone in framing that definition.

On our first travels we'd floated on whim, spores adrift, blending clouds of love as we learned each other's tongues and conjugated our own idiom. This time Greece took us three months to work through, Turkey the same, Thailand almost six. Researcher, photographer, translator, writer, we packed our laptops everywhere each day, yet my handwriting filled one notebook after another. I scrambled to move the pen fast enough.

These travels were bliss encore.

In airports and libraries I met magazines. Narratives went into my laptop and out again, as submissions. Rejection wasn't defeat. In nature, most attempts at distribution fail. Only if many occur do some succeed.

The first anniversary of this happy life found us in Malaysia with a bevy of lichenologists. At the hotel, after collecting the colloquium's agenda and our mail, we panted up to our room for air-conditioned love, but found that Mrs. Whatsit had sent photos.

"She looks like you," in unison.

Shiny coloured rectangles slid over the king-size. She held a toy plane Lawrence had sent her from Istanbul. On Mrs. Whatsit's lap she cuddled smiling, on my father's too.

"A lot like you," we repeated. I told the truth.

When he thought I wouldn't notice, Lawrence examined the photos again, again. I heard his fingers handling *them,* not notes or reports. He tried to bring the images into bed. I wouldn't agree. He persisted. I ...sed a new rule arriving. When he reached for me I was sure, and quickly moved to my own margin. By now I understood my mother's twin bed. She had no notebooks, though, poor woman. Then and there in front of Lawrence I got out my stories and began to write in my own idiom.

He did not ask. He, we did not speak our language *very much any more* (another conundrum for the translators).

Her third birthday approached. Lawrence wanted to go to Canada.

"What would a child that age know about celebration?"

He had no scientific comeback, but one day after a siege of meetings he and I were having drinks with other participants. A fellow translator asked me with gentle concern if I were tired.

Lawrence snapped, "No, Ellen always slouches like that. And she gets all worked up."

The inquirer stammered. Others lowered their eyes while my husband publicly raged, glared, sulked.

At last I said I'd go. Not then. At Christmas. With conditions. Our arrival must be unannounced, so no airport reunion. No gambols, no funny gifts of the kind that Mrs. Whatsit, given opportunity, would invent. And we'd stay at a downtown hotel, to prevent a child from slipping into our room at dawn expecting special treatment.

I had to force myself to get on the plane. Even my parents' rather austere seasonal practices reared up like penitentiary walls. (That's the last, unless I've lost count. Four's plenty.)

At dusk the taxi moved through softly falling white to the old neighbourhood and so to the Whatsits' house, its basement dark. Snow flowed around us.

Peering through the bright living-room window, we saw our daughter, arms akimbo, face red, tongue stuck out. Her body shook with shouting, "No no no, I hate you!" Tears sprang off her face.

Lawrence gasped, laughed. His eyes too were wet.

My mother-in-law, her back to us, spoke inaudibly. Her hair was greyer. She was fifty-five now, I calculated.

"When the worst teen years hit, she'll just be getting her pension."

Lawrence's fist almost reached me, but we flinched. That idiom, alien still. We watched as the woman and child calmed down, smiled, kissed.

He and I kissed too, a long deep final word. Then the father ran up to his front door.

I walked, wondering where under the everywhere whiteness lay that delicate lichen, frilled, leathery.

Through the living-room window of my parents' house glinted an enormous Christmas tree. For her. They never used to do that. A light shone in the attic, another by my private door. My key slid in. On the stairs I sat to note the essentials. In the airport lounge I'd go further, for likely there'd be hours before the flight above the tumbling snow, hours to live in my idiom. Ours no more. Never hers.

Some women take to it, some don't.

Writing poetry was now imaginable.

I tiptoed up.

My parents' huge TV and chairs and beds were in the attic, as were they, two tiny dried-apple dolls in robes and slippers by the fire. They nibbled mince-tarts. On the dormer windows, glittering lichen bonded with the sky. The trees, sheathed in ice, stood silent.

My mother sighed. "So nice with just the two of us."

"What did you say?"

Dirty Work

WITH DEEPEST SYMPATHY?
In Your Hour of Loss?
Certainly not.

I searched through the rack of cards with no text. Flowers and rivers cooled both the September heat and my anger at the day's news reports from Afghanistan about Bush at his dirty work again, cosying up to the Taliban's leaders. Stars, clouds, ocean beaches.

Then—a wide field where two old trees stood close, their colours muted, the sage and olive conveying respect, I thought. Admiration.

Rowena deserves neither. Light and lethal as plastic wrap she is, so I bought that card. *Very sorry to hear the news. Catherine.* She'll get it. With snail mail you can't see recipients react, though, unless your daily lives are linked. Perhaps she never noticed that ours briefly were.

Entering the Vancouver branch thirty years ago, Rowena wore an ankle-length coat, black wool. Richard walked behind, royal consort. She was tall, pale; the fashionable coat gave her still more height and presence. This twenty-something pair were fresh to the Coast, had just driven his old beater cross-country from the movement's Centre in Toronto. Who forked over for that garment? Not Ms. Radical, who never had a nickel for the collection bucket. Her man was taller, paler, with a curly smile, and bent to Rowena like a folding measuring-stick. They wore Beatles glasses. His long hair was carroty red, hers a stream of black.

Sally, the assistant organizer, stood no chance. Her stocky build would have made that coat grotesque, and her face—after years of poverty, fluorescent light, cheap food, the stress of political crises—was sallow mud. Organizer Pete's skin was as coarse. Unimportant, for an important man. Nor did his hands matter, stained by Gestetner, silk-screen, spirit ditto, Remington and Underwood. He and Sally exuded the twinnish affect of the long-coupled. Pals.

Cordially they brought the new comrades to the hall's kitchen for the Friday supper, and sat by them: Sally, Richard, Rowena, Pete. I was there, only a contact, not seated by the leaders, but I too saw Pete draw on the paper table-cover a map of downtown. As Rowena watched, his ballpoint showed the route for the anti-war march coming up in April 1971.

"See?"

"You're the chief marshal?" Admiring gaze. Wide eyes. The works.

Pete blushed.

Richard's death thirty years later, a week ago: sad. Not tragic, like those of others once in the movement, Josie, Bruce.

In today's newspaper, tomorrow's, Richard wouldn't rate a line of print, but last week the *Sun* did note yet another drunk driver's kill: male, 55, credit union manager. No family mentioned. Local TV showed a rainy crosswalk. Diagonally across the white stripes, a reflective yellow jacket. Long legs scissoring. A crushed bike.

Right after Richard and Rowena's arrival on the Coast, anti-war worked hard to build the protest against America's war in Vietnam. What *hard* means, people unfamiliar with radical politics have no idea. Friends of mine do time in the standard parties, but even if angry, worn out, tricked of victory, they're safe. Secure. The left that *I* knew felt itself alone on a shattering rim.

That march was a huge success, Vancouver's biggest to date, the cops nearly brutal. Seventeen seconds on *The National.*

At the movement's social that night (the hall antic with exhausted revelry), the assistant organizer located me in the crowded half-dark. *The Age of Aquarius* reverberated so that Sally had to repeat her question.

"Cathy, could you find space for a comrade?"

"*Catherine*. I don't understand?"

She explained. How humiliating.

My apartment then had an odd ell off the hallway where I stored camping gear.

"Of course!"

Sally obviously wanted to leave at once. I had no one to stay for. Silent, she walked by me down the hill towards the West End, where freighters' lights glinted on English Bay's blackness. The mountains, invisible.

At my place, as we cleared away tent and paddles to roll out foam and sleeping bag, I accidentally touched her arm. Tense. Almost rigid.

The next week, two small cartons and a suitcase appeared. The revolutionary stored her food in a corner of the fridge and washed her few dishes right away.

"I'll be gone by month's end," paying her share of the rent to the penny.

Why did Sally ask a contact for refuge? Not a comrade. Not even a former comrade who'd dropped to sympathizer. Among the latter, old Duncan had heroic status, having gone to Spain with the Mac-Pap brigade. Others had cachet if they'd continued radical work in unions or the NDP, but most were judged as simply having failed to cut the mustard.

In Vancouver as elsewhere, thousands came *around* the far-left in the 1960s, 70s. Some were just *here on a visit,* as the comrades said, but others lasted over a decade, into the death years. I did. Rowena was soon history, off to write her dirty work—aka gossip columns—for any paying rag, but Richard, another relict, kept on through turn and fusion, faction and split, all the while studying accountancy.

Those two trees on that greeting card—why alone? Logging? Fire?

Ten decades ago, where I live was little more than tracks hacked out of ancient forest. A paddler by the shore, once past the False Creek sawmills, would have seen little through the trees but wisps of wood-stove smoke. Now it's all towers and traffic.

Not long after Sally came to my place, on returning from a late movie I heard moans in the ell. Walk by, brush teeth, bed. A strangled concluding gasp. The apartment door closed, the street door. Out my room's window I saw a comrade walk away.

Next morning, Sally and I stapled some beach-towels into a curtain to shield the open end of her space.

Some of the almost nightly men were comrades, one a leading trade unionist and friend of Pete's. This trophy pleased me. Where she got the others I don't know. None stayed over. Sally then was thirty-five, I a decade older. Did she, wrongly, believe herself still young? At her age I failed to detach a man from his marriage. A pretty woman succeeded. No later chances at a long-term connection came my way. As for Rowena, she could have been my daughter.

What did we contacts do? What comrades did: cook Friday suppers, staff the bar at socials, distribute leaflets, paint banners, address envelopes, put up posters, sell newspapers, drive (few comrades had cars) to the demo, the printer, post office, bus depot, union hall, women's centre, airport, ferry terminal, liquor store, hospital. We donated toilet and typing and carbon paper, paper towels, paper for silkscreening. We gave cash. What we couldn't do: participate in the branch to decide the line.

My first act of witness occurred while on an errand at the Courthouse.

On its legal steps stood perhaps a dozen people, in chilly rain. *Stop the War in Vietnam*, their placards demanded. Alone they stood, held, were stared at. Thus I learned that my small hatred of America's invasion wasn't unique.

My notary's office, my cubby, overlooked False Creek. Weeks later those same people, a twig of the Fourth International's Canadian section, rented space downstairs. The storefront window advertised their forums, also meetings of a local anti-war group. I went. Again, again.

Having been in my thirties still imprisoned by hopes of marriage, I'd only seen on TV the huge *Ban the Bomb* marches surge over Burrard Bridge, Now I began to live in the vigour of anti-war. The slogans grew nuanced, transitional: *End Canada's Complicity, Bring the Troops Home, Don't Do Uncle Sam's Dirty Work*. Clean bombs, dirty: that distinction featured in 50s war-talk too, then in the 80s, 90s.

The language of the 00s won't differ. Today that's beyond doubt. *Dirty work. Someone's got to do it.*

Another, later discovery and distinction: I opposed all war. The comrades didn't.

Professionally I did little for the branch. In British Columbia we're scrivener notaries, with more powers than in many other jurisdictions, but revolutionaries don't redeem stocks and bonds or purchase real estate overseas—not that I frequently oversaw such tasks. Often, notaries just witness. (That again.) *This person is who she claims to be. This document does what it purports to do.* Law school hadn't been an option. I got over that; most people change shape to fit. I did review the branch's lease with Pete, and gave advice after Maoists smashed the print-room window, but a lawyer was needed when two Youth got charged with resisting arrest.

Once I did assist children of the revolution. An anguished narrative of cross-border separation, separation, separation, divorce, illness, death, grief preceded these relicts. The extant parent needed a notary to satisfy US authorities that certain monies could be paid to the youths, or, in one case, to the parent in trust. All the real decisions long predated that amputated family's arrival in my cubby.

The organizer and assistant organizer, Pete and Sally, side by side for years before *The Age of Aquarius* dawned, though uprooted by Rowena still must confer. Avoiding their private office, they worked at a card table in the main hall. Low voices. Eyes on file-folders. Nearby, a work-party collated a pamphlet critiquing social democracy. Even we contacts knew that Sally'd asked the Centre for a transfer to Edmonton, Windsor, anywhere.

A chair banged to the floor, a high-speed hand met a face.

Sally rushed out.

We picked up page three, four. Pete didn't touch his flaming cheek. The stapler bit sets of sheets. He folded the card table, went to the office, shut the door. Dialling. Soon, a honk in the back alley. He left. We finished our assignment.

Even with my bedroom door closed, I heard Sally and the man.

What did all that fucking mean? With Pete, had the basics of release, satisfaction, been rare? So easy to despise another thoughtless man whose cock makes his life-choices—yet Sally's sex at my place did seem *routinist*, the movement's term for one kind of political thought and action. A clinical assessment: nearly dead. They arrived about half-past eleven, she and someone, when the news was over and I'd finished in the bathroom. Soft footsteps. Flushes. Murmurs. Darkness, stillness, then the sounds.

After some nights of regret I'd been so accommodating, of wishing my guests would hurry up and be done with it so we could all get some sleep, I found my own breasts tingling. To touch myself with others nearby, unaware, was novel. Exciting. I stuffed the sheet's hem in my mouth. My body became more eager, until when they entered my place I'd already be in bed, lights out, my hands moving. To keep myself from coming till at least one of them did was a painful pleasure.

I slept well. Sally's morning face was porridge-grey, her shoulders curled as if to block further injury to her core.

Satisfaction. Is that what I felt last week, shoving Rowena's envelope in the mailbox? Even at seventy-five, I don't know.

Perhaps it's me who wants condolences, sympathy for not being the relict of an old pair with dead roots still strong, romantic.

On Fridays before the forums, Sally with Pete still welcomed everyone to supper, she as ever a little shy, he affable. During his post-movement years with NGOs in Zimbabwe and Kenya, that trait surely served Pete well.

At the meal itself he sat by Rowena.

Sally, her back to them, chose another table.

Pale Richard ate anywhere. His eyelids had the rusty edges, sore-looking, that some redheads get, and he communed with his chili or hash as if in a room where no other steps sounded. I know that room. He didn't converse. I and others tried, more than once.

During dessert, Pete rose to announce upcoming events. One night came great news: a French comrade, direct from the International, would expand his North American speaking itinerary to include our outpost.

Such a buzz over the canned pears!

Sally got up also, unusually, to remind us that North America's struggle too was crucial for world revolution. As always, correct. Yet who'd choose to hear postal worker Helen on mechanization's threat, again, when with Raoul we'd enter French anti-war? Helen was no Jeanne Moreau. In our heads 1968 still shimmered. Aznavour, Belmondo. We contacts, no matter our age and the pears' tinny taste, just then felt part of *us*.

Those tragic deaths.

Josie. Only seventeen, she asked such urgent and politically naive questions that the Youth snickered. Older comrades winced, kept a kind eye. In a matter of weeks her speech fragmented. A brain tumour lopped off her life.

Saplings planted alongside city sidewalks often wear necklaces. *Please water me.* For all its rain, this climate may not provide enough. Some don't survive. During winter, dead young trees look just like live ones. The surprise comes in April.

Near those trees on Rowena's card was there a river, a wriggle of blue?

Comrade Bruce was forty-five but took the split hard, a child of bitter political divorce. Less than a year later he was running drugs across the Montana-Alberta border. A train killed him. His last joe-job for the International had been to remove the bright posters, banners, placards from the storefront.

The empty hall: unbearable.

A friend of mine, a commissioner of oaths, had found a spacious office in Gastown, above a typewriter shop, and suggested we share.

In 1990, a thousand affidavits later, Claudia and I retired from witnessing how rough human existence is, how knotty, contaminated.

Gladly, the computer store beneath expanded into our space. Such limited powers each of us has. Now Claudia and other friends and I sit around our dinner tables, shocked at how little time remains. Some men, lovers, husbands, are already gone. Fewer places are set. The past looks impenetrable, like islands as a kayak moves away; individual landforms coalesce into one dark shape, no visible channels in.

Why did so many contacts not turn into comrades?

Cowardice.

Fear of democratic centralism: *Join that group, Carry this line.*

Dues. Some people won't spend even on what's important to them.

Me? I couldn't accept *The end justifies the means* and *By any means necessary*, i.e. violence. All the Romanovs needn't have died. Nor the Kronstadt sailors. To give only two examples. No doubt the comrade assigned long ago to *have a serious political talk with Cathy* (repeatedly I had to claim my full name) made her report. Written off as a liberal, I thought as I pleased while newly alive in anti-war pickets, marches, vigils, tribunals organized by Trotskyists alone or with other groups on hard-won bases of unity sometimes narrow, sometimes broad.

Ten years ago, as the US did its filthy work in Iraq and the ground war began, Vancouver's February streets filled again, differently: *Operation Desert Storm.*

Amid thronging youth walked relicts like me, *surviving from a previous age or in changed circumstances after the disappearance of related forms, species, structures.* Bald Richard, wheeling his bicycle along the route from the Main Street train station to the once-Courthouse, told me of his volunteer work repairing bikes in the Downtown East Side. As the bullhorns assembled, I turned to say, "Shall we get out of here?" But he'd already taken a pass on the orations.

A puzzle, that 1991 meeting with Richard. He didn't seem an apparition from a distant past. I already knew (how?) that he'd worked at a credit union. At some point after the far left imploded in the late 70s and before the Gulf invasion, he and I must have met. I don't remember.

Later in the 90s he turned up at the local farmers' market, smiling as he bent to show customers his loaves of rye and seedy bread. Occasionally I buy from Richard. Bought. We'd chat, as friendly relicts do. Homeward with organic this and that along the flowering streets, I'd speculate. Which causes most harm—cruelty, thoughtlessness, meaning well?

To accommodate Raoul, the French Trotskyist, an entire month of forums had been rescheduled. He—a short, plain man, the first disappointment—came to the hall with Pete and Sally the evening before his talk.

Just then comrades and contacts were doing a mailing about the Caravan to Ottawa planned by Vancouver's women's liberation: a cross-country drive to the capital, en route gathering supporters to demand changes in the abortion laws. A Great Trek, as in the 30s. Something big could happen. Everyone sensed that. Mass action, even. We folded leaflets, stuffed envelopes.

The task brought me as close to the sisterhood as I ever got. Yes, I'd attended some meetings of independent WL groups. The girls—no, young women—were friendly, but because of work I couldn't stay up late on weeknights, nor could I sit on the floor as they did for hours, talking. Already it wasn't easy to kneel for a full morning's paddle in a canoe. Also my hair was permed. I wore heels and suits and a girdle and a sturdy bra. A living fossil. Now I'll admit that their sexual exuberance intimidated me. Nothing to be done about that, then or now.

After introducing Raoul, Pete and Sally left for an external meeting. She walked out first, looking back as if puzzled he wasn't at her side. Only when she reached the street door did he follow.

The Frenchman helped us, efficiently, and in spite of his exoticism the atmosphere soon normalized. He learned some names (not mine), asked about local women's politics and anti-war, but the conversation jolted. His English was far from fluent. We had to rephrase, oversimplify. I hoped he planned to read his speech.

Our work done, Raoul yawned, smiled. "I'd so much wish to ski while at Vancouver!"

Silence. *Ski! How bourgeois!* Not among French revolutionaries, evidently.

Pete and Sally never even headed out to camp, paddle, hike. Never drove to Seattle for a weekend. Rarely saw a movie. However, some of my friends skied. I went cross-country myself occasionally, though I've always loved liquid water best.

My voice sounded. "Rowena might drive you up to Cypress."

By coincidence she arrived in the hall soon after, long coat swaying, hair shining. Now, in the photo heading Rowena's theatre column and in her spreads on glamorous Down syndrome and lupus fundraisers, her hair's still black. She's only mid-fifties, though. Dye won't yet cause that awful stiffness characteristic of hollow white hairs.

"Of course!" Lightly, smiling.

After this foray I was breathless.

The next night, Raoul stood before an overflow audience. He glanced at Rowena. To me she was in profile, eyes unseen, but I'd have bet a month's income on the quality of her gaze. Sally introduced the speaker. His smiling thanks, so patronizing: handsome male to plain female. Anger ran me up and down. Already fired with joy at what I'd instigated, I sensed a sudden all-over heat and for a while heard nothing.

When sound began again, the atmosphere had gone wrong. Everyone lay open to the delights of political seduction, but that Frenchman, so expert and experienced, just hadn't the tongue. We weren't inside French anti-war. We were nowhere special. Fidgets, coughs. Flirtatiously, Raoul glanced at Sally for help. Once, twice, she supplied an English word or phrases. Then quit. Stared.

Before the reception began, Sally left the building.

That storefront.

For years, I walked blocks out of my way. Since the comrades vacated it's beckoned passersby to a hair salon, commercial real estate, now a travel agency. Some arcane evangelical sect uses the main hall and kitchen. Even now, nostalgia's poison streaks the air. I dip and dodge. Often those who appear aren't the *hardened bureaucratic layer* but the dead, or crazy Nora, or Richard, tossed aside.

After the Frenchman limped to his conclusion, in the loud hall I glimpsed Rowena as I drained my Gallo red. Serpent to vermin, she neared Raoul. He hadn't noticed her yet, didn't see me. I was getting my coat when Pete passed me. Such a vulnerable look. Then Duncan took him by the arm. To shove the old boy aside, cross the hall, pull his love Rowena close. . . No. For the organizer of revolution, impossible.

Serve him right. That breathlessness again, born of making something bleed and writhe. Something to itself huge: a worm a bug a belief a love.

Not just a middle-aged single self-employed notary who'd sensed her body's first helpless waver towards menopause, I walked home. Red glowed on the beach, illicit bonfires. Beyond lay the night-filled park, where thousands of trees grow unrestrained except by storms or fire. Unseen, mountains tower behind. From first light they dominate. As for the land, if you're even a little way out from shore its curves and wrinkles flatten, disappear.

With old eyes it's hard to be sure what's still there, what never was.

As I opened my apartment door, Sally lunged at me.

"How dare you do that to Pete? Hurt him so?"

I nearly fell over her suitcase.

"What gives *you* the right to sic that woman on to Raoul?"

She varied her queries, making each *s* a hiss. Response wasn't permitted.

"You're as bad as her." Sally grabbed her case.

"Where will you go?"

"Nowhere you know about."

Slam.

I still get the radical press, such as it is, and read recently of Raoul's demise at sixty-eight. He'd stuck with the Fourth International in that distant Centre far more central than Toronto, New York even. Imperial.

As for Sally, her photo often appears in press coverage of public sector unions. On TV through the 90s she critiqued NAFTA. Clear, capable. Her term as union president ends soon. In retirement she'll learn how fast work drops away, abandons us.

I was her Samaritan. She could fuck nearby because I, unreal, couldn't notice. Also I had no one to tell. The beach-towels we hung up? Fiction. By acting as I did, I'd come off the page.

Thirty years ago Sally left me alone to contemplate her love and scorn. She headed down the street, thence rapidly to Fredericton. Later, Halifax. Thus she missed Friday supper the week following Raoul's talk.

Pete was absent too, at a film about British colonialism in Africa. Did that start his trajectory from revolution? Today he's an aid consultant in Ottawa.

As I cleared dirty plates and brought clean ones, the cracked timbre of Duncan's voice went on and on about Spain. Rowena listened.

"Could you draw it? I'd love to see what you did!"

Duncan pushed his coffee away, got out a pencil.

Though his eyes watered, his hand sketching the battle-scene moved confidently.

"We were here." He put *x x x* near his coffee cup, then not far off some clusters of o o o o o o. "They were there. 1938."

"You were in charge?" That admiring gaze.

"Yes." The pencil fell. "So many died." He stared at his marks.

Richard spooned up his raspberry Jello.

That night Helen spoke on postal mechanization.

Every danger that plain Cassandra foresaw, every lost deskilled devalued job, was realized in two decades. Once, mail sorters scanned handwritten envelopes by the thousand, tossed them at high pigeonholes so fast the air blurred white. Encyclopedic urban knowledge, emptied out of human brains.

Next afternoon the Caravan departed.

Before the Courthouse another small group, all women this time, excited, nervy, smoking, flaring into laughter. The shouting cars, bright with painted slogans, headed off to Ottawa and history. That autumn the War Measures Act would refill the plaza, chop off yet another past and force everyone to breathe differently.

Later in the 70s I found an apartment nearer the park. I watch tides, try to remember.

In September 2001, why on earth would Rowena see herself as a tree? *Catherines* abound; to her my name will signal nothing. Nor does my tiny hate, except it's the same as the huge ones. We're all relicts now.

If I could go back thirty years to that hall, would I recognize anyone?

That question went to bed with me yesterday after hours of televised filthy clouds, rage, wreckage, wild faces, distorted or disassembled bodies, hours of phone calls repeating many words.

When I woke in a later darkness, my head said *Grenada. Richard.*

In 1983 the US used the pretext of Maurice Bishop's assassination to invade the island, with *Operation Urgent Fury* the attack's codename. During a quickly organized protest at the American consulate, some placards riffed on that, *Operation Urgent Withdrawal, Urgent End Imperialist Attack.* Richard and I had both made signs reading *US Out of Grenada Now.*

It was good to see him. His red hair was already greying, thinner. I asked how he liked working at VanCity.

"I've always wanted to be part of a community. How are you, Catherine?"

He knew my name.

"Do you miss the old days, Richard? The movement?"

The demo was only sporadic chanting in front of American plate glass coated to exclude the world's eyes, so we talked. We remembered Josie, Bruce. We noted Pete's job in Kenya, Sally's steady rise in her union. I wouldn't have mentioned Rowena.

"Aren't her columns fun?" That curly smile. "Good for her, too, letting people know about these causes."

Grenada: eighteen years ago. Under what beach-towel did I conceal Richard's forgiveness?

To sleep again this morning, impossible. The vile screen required witness.

This afternoon my condolence card waited in my mailbox, with Scotch tape over the flap, Rowena's address inked out, mine inserted. That meadow is broader than in memory, the sky more spacious, soaring even. No fiery planes. Past tall rushes, a little stream winds who knows where. One old tree leans to the other as Richard did to her, loving, eager to hear.

I put no return address on the envelope. Rowena's dug it, me, up somewhere. She's remembered, even if she didn't scribble *Fuck you Cathy* or *Go to hell*.

Ha!

Got to her though, didn't I?

Made her mad.

The Hunter

IF THE CAT STRETCHED TILL SHE HURT, her front paws reached the bars on one side and the tip of her long black-ringed tail, thick and plushy, touched the other side.

He'd constructed the steel cage for her sight unseen, a cube, five-sided, and lapped wire mesh all round. It resembled a parcel. His present. Pretty arrived tranquillized, in a plastic travelling container; he decanted her beauty into the cage as if pouring cake mix into a pan. The fit pleased him. Her body was three feet long, her tail another three. All over, the oily exudate of his Pretty's fur coated the mesh.

She didn't see sharply but had little to observe. A windowless basement room, pale featureless gyproc. One door to a bathroom, another to stairs. In the cage, a metal stool. Early on, she used it as a change from lying or pacing, now only when he ran the hose. For water, a metal cake pan. At the beginning of their shared life his Pretty often knocked it about, *clash bang ring!* He worked hard, needed sleep. Couldn't she tell night from day by the rhythms of the house's lighting systems? Would she adapt? Now the pan stayed still.

The wire mesh made for easy clambering. The green video had shown Pretty's superb climbing skills, and for toys he'd provided knobs and rings of tough plastic. They lay still. He shook his head. Here she was, acquired at such cost and risk, safe and warm and fed and cleaned-up after and talked to, yet her eyes always angled off. To what? When he put her food through the slot he might shout, or slap the cage. If she startled, he got a moment's satisfaction.

As to flooring, he'd thought wire mesh would be uncomfortable, so bolted the cage into the concrete below smooth industrial linoleum. Her pads wore an X-trail and one round the edge. She scratched the lino, stained it too, the acids of her excretions corroding the surface while he worked or slept or watched teenaged Asian girls masturbate. His Pretty came already spayed, of course. Shreds of meat got mushed about the floor, too. Drinking, she slopped. Every day he hosed down her living quarters, then ran heat lamps and fans. She developed a cough. Inaudibly, pain shot up her legs from beneath the concrete, from the deep cold midden studded with millennia of clam and oyster shells. The room smelled of her.

Sometimes his Pretty lay dead-still, a limp tumble of tawny, ochre, silver-grey, black. His heart thumped until under the supple skin he detected a throb. He'd jiggle the steel pins securing her food-slot. Could she resist?

Never quite. A small victory, but often she didn't bother to get up, or ate little, even if he'd on purpose delayed a feeding.

Above her, in the rest of the rented house, flourished hundreds of plants, their lushness suggesting the green video of her homeland. During the years of saving and planning and fear that at last brought his Pretty, he'd watched the images repeatedly, learned her special name, *neofelis nebulosa*. With her sibs, Pretty frolicked enticingly to expose the stunning black ovals on her belly. That vision gave him strength.

As Mumma taught, he made a list: (1) get passport; (2) buy plastic containers for cake; (3) leave Vancouver for the first time ever, to hunt his clouded leopard and bring her home. He didn't learn that she'd entered the world on a Texas game ranch. Soon after he'd placed his online order, nearly fainting as he logged out (*What have you done, son?*), his cellphone rang. Obedient, he drove the van to Bellingham. No one asked to see his passport, and he'd only needed one plastic cake-container. Ten cakes had fitted in the pack he'd bought for the much longer hunt expected, in that green Nepalese forest.

As for the cannabis, his skill ensured that the plants' exposure to light was shortened every twenty-four hours by the right number of minutes, that measured fertilizer was applied at the most fruitful moment, that water arrived constantly, that useless foliage got plucked off just when buds would thirstily absorb the resulting surge of nutrients. Capacitors, switches, transformers, drip-lines, timers—for all, he was accountable. Orderly and dutiful, he did a good job. Mumma would have to agree.

Grow lights intensified the plants' rank scent. Other odours formed as drywall, carpet, hardwood responded with mould to the hydroponics. The humid air bore also vanilla, chocolate, orange, butterscotch, for daily he baked up a cake mix. No other groceries were stored in the house, but his takeout Greek, Mexican, and Chinese enriched the diverse gases moving through his Pretty's lungs. Her own food, picked up in the van from a wholesale butcher, lay in a large freezer.

During harvest, he'd seen her waver, even stagger. Was she stoned? Sick? The latter option he never dwelled on; nothing could be done. But if only she were more lively! One twitch showed off her coat's extravagant patterns. He longed to glimpse that splendour while taking a break from his lonely work, but she lay still, still, her rather short stocky legs splayed out. She never climbed to her roof any more. So. Again. The old agenda: (1) strip the plants; (2) bag them; (3) at night, carry the heavy plastic sacks out to the van; (4) drive them to their destination (obeying all the rules of the road, he was never pulled over); (5) replant.

Nine harvests thus. The limit, for security's sake, of his and Pretty's tenure, but he wanted to break the rule and stay. To move her cage, make her home cleaner, nicer.

So neighbours wouldn't wonder about the blind house, he mowed the lawn, set out garbage, cleared gutters. One week children's toys and bikes lay on the front steps, the next week at the back. He parked the well-washed van properly. Inside, while grow lights gulped power off the grid in staggering amounts, he maintained strict surveillance on all mechanical systems. He scraped incipient black mould off the carpet, using Mumma's old-fashioned vinegar mix, never bleach, in case of contamination.

Each individual plant, luxuriant, purplish, viridian, was known to him, and he adjusted the gifts of fertilizer by sixteenths of a teaspoon. First-class and abundant product resulted. Mumma couldn't criticize.

His masters, busy with their profits, acquiesced. "Okay, one more year." Unlike some of their grow-ops, the retard's caused no trouble.

Pretty now ate so erratically that drugging her food wouldn't be a reliable precaution. To move the cage, therefore, he made a list. (1) drill new holes in the concrete, check the new plants, bake; (2) loosen and remove the present bolts; (3) lift and tug the cage's lowest bar, now held down so tightly it indented the lino; (4) push the cage, Pretty inside, to the new site; (6) insert and tighten the bolts in their new location, check the plants; (5) eat brownies and watch the special TV girl, the winking girl with the sliding hands.

During (3), could a paw slide under the cage? Doubtful. Maybe so. He rehearsed frequently the necessary motions of arms, legs, hands. How smoothly Pretty would travel!

Drilling the new bolt-holes made a dreadful noise, though, and concrete dust fogged the basement room. In distress, Pretty folded back her soft round ears—he'd never seen that. She paced, coughing hard.

"I'm sorry, Pretty." He opened the bathroom window and went upstairs. For each new crop he set up the lighting system from scratch, again, and for the hydroponics he checked each pump and switch and gauge. If he found he'd missed one, he started over. Good job. While nestling the seedlings in their containers, his fingers practiced in miniature the grips, hoists, and shoves to come with (2) and (3). His Pretty would blink gold. Gobble her food, lick her paws. Maybe to sleep she'd curl up sweetly in the way he loved, her long tail wrapped all round.

All was well.

Now the brownie mix. He never used drugs, despised the smokers who threw away their lives on fantasies. The pan in the oven, he set the timer and adjusted the fan. The homey fragrance would vent outside, reassuringly meet a neighbour's nose. Ahead now lay an hour's work, max. Pretty's clouds would shimmer. Might he touch them? Once or twice, indifferent, she'd paced so near the mesh that softness met his fingertips.

When he dropped the first freed bolt, Pretty raised her elegant head, sat up as he moved from one face of the cage to the next. Her glorious tail rippled. Alert, she watched the wrench, watched him shuffling on his knees from bolt to bolt, as if praying. Mumma always prayed. He didn't any more. Did she know? Pretty stretched her neck out, stared. Her whiskers, barely sketched wings, moved as she sought his purpose.

He'd got all the bolts loose. Out.

Now the quick sharp lift-and-tug.

Done! All that needless anxiety over. Good job.

Now lean and push. Push. He grimaced, his cheeks heated, he smelled chocolate, and slowly the container shunted across the ravaged lino. His Pretty, as the cage distanced itself from her on one side and neared her on the other, sat peering on her metal stool. Then she got down to pad about her voyaging prison, not in her usual tranced trudge, but curiously.

The metal cake pan tipped over. He and Pretty startled. She lapped at the spilled water, batted at the pan so it flew up to the cage's ceiling and fell, flew and fell. *Clatter ring bang!* Her play made his heart glad. A few more pushes, to line the cage up with the new bolt-holes. *Neofelis nebulosa* now licked a paw, extended and retracted her claws, blinked. Her lashes: tiny gold feathers.

Movement stopped. What? One leg of the stool had lodged in an abandoned bolt-hole. The stool, jammed against a corner, braked the cage.

Shake, bang. No good. Leverage, yes, but the tire iron was too big to go through the mesh, the plastic tubing from the grow-rooms too light. Pretty patted at it, gave a small jump. From her throat rose a resonance. Her kind of cat didn't purr, he knew, but the noise sounded happy.

The kitchen timer rang.

Eating hot brownies hadn't been on the list, but he needed energy. No fork, Mumma would fuss. Her knitting needles, they'd be perfect. Wiggle one to distract, the other to shake that stool loose. Perfect knitting, never a dropped stitch. He put the half-empty pan back in the oven to stay warm and got calves' liver from the freezer. To his Pretty, cooked food was even worse than dead, so as soon as the blood-smell rose he took the meat from the microwave.

The revised list: (1) use the toilet; (2) barely open the cage door and fling the liver across it; (3) reach in with the tire iron to dislodge the stool.

Attending to (1), his bowels were loose and foul. Nerves. (2) went well, with Pretty sniffing the meat all over. For (3) he rehearsed the sequence of movements. Her glance at him was golden.

Five seconds, a scream and a crack of bone, an empty cage. Mumma's knitting needle, somehow, stuck out of his leg. Agony. His cellphone, as far off as Texas or Nepal, on the kitchen counter. Even if, whom to call? Communication with the masters was one-way. And he'd forgotten to turn off the oven. Carbonized chocolate, venting to the world.

He let go into pain. Psychedelic visions of the grow-rooms, green and lush, heralded glimpses of his kitten padding through her jungle, dapples melting in leaves and light. Rapidly, the filth from Pretty's claws inflamed the wounds on his face and arms.

In seconds, the cat had entered the bathroom's stench.

Two more, to identify the source of fresh air.

Eleven to leap from the tub's rim to the sill and squeeze her head and front paws through and scrabble her strong hindquarters up and balance her weight and launch into darkness, tail flying out behind.

Three jumps took her across the grow-op's weedless back lawn. A slide to cover, under a rhododendron in the next-door garden. Thin leathery leaves festooned its branches, fallen ones lay on the cold ground.

A long scrambling rush took her, running low under fences and through hedges, to the end of the block. Under a Japanese maple she crouched, smelling, but the need for height was urgent. She leapt to a Douglas fir and went thirty feet up.

Since her escape, ninety seconds. She coughed.

Two dogs barked. A door opened.

In midnight terror, wings scissored away from the fir.

The cat sniffed water. Underground water, rain coming, salt. Animal fur, droppings, spray. Humans. Plants grasses bushes. Dead leaves loose, crackling, mashed, skeletal. Fish, shellfish, algae. Stiff bull-kelp on the stony beaches. Insects, their acid odours. Powdery bird-feathers. Bird-shit. A rabbit, decomposing. Insecticides, herbicides, pesticides. Also diesel, sulphur, fuel oil, hot metal, sawdust, transmission fluid, chlorine, gasoline, tar, rendering plant, concrete batch plant, wheat, logs, milled lumber, rubber, paint thinner, creosote—in billions, the molecules floated by.

Over there, that way, she smelled a density of trees. Something mechanical honked on the ocean. A dog got hauled indoors. Bright lights shone amid a thousand shadows. Fast-moving clouds spattered the heavens while a new moon appeared, vanished, again made the water glitter. Closer by, window lights, door lights, street lights. Someone rummaged through a garbage can and a yard light flashed on.

Restless, the cat moved up the fir. More birds flew. A bark. Stretched out, she let the Pacific northwest fill her damaged lungs and coat her palate. Down to the roots of her exceptionally long canines the flavours penetrated, entered her digestive tract to unite with her. The November night parted the hairs of her coat, drawing off the stench of cannabis, dead cow, human feces. She shivered. When clouds next covered the moon, she ran down the tree head-first.

In her exquisite camouflage she moved slow and smoky as a plume from a dying bonfire. Her pads silenced gravel, and a tabby kitten out exploring his night garden hadn't a chance. His spinal cord cracked like celery, his punctured windpipe hissed. To eat, she dragged her catch into massed periwinkle. Around his neck looped a revolting thing. She tore his head off and moved her meal away from the circlet.

Down hill now, every sense thrilling. She coughed.

Between her and that far wooded darkness lay a barrier of brilliant noise. Back and forth the cat trotted by the highway. No choice. Only across. To gain her moment, she crouched on a guardrail. One trucker took her for a dog, what breed? Another, home on the prairies days later, told his son about a golden-grey monkey near the ocean.

She whimpered, rushed.

Safe, in a jungle of salal, salmonberry, morning-glory all wound through with tunnels, she went eastwards. Rats and mice stopped heart-still, sensing her amid dirty diapers, syringes, beer bottles, toasters, pop cans, condoms, rotting mattresses, rusted cylinders of hairspray and Lysol. She glided on. By the railway tracks, puddles blanched under sodium lights, and the water had a harsh savour. Coughing, she tasted her own blood. Cinders stuck between her toes. Now soothing grasses, stiff and dead, whose hissing rustle masked her passage. Nearer the beach, saplings offered cover. The tide was coming in. She padded over rip-rap and driftwood, sniffed at shells and a dead crab. She urinated, defecated, scratched at the sand to cover and trotted back into the tall grass, head low, haunches high.

The park's swimming pool, drained after Thanksgiving, had been replenished by rain. The water shimmered. Over the chain-link fence she flowed, her dapples interlacing with moonlight. Widgeons and mergansers took squawking flight, one mallard was too slow. Although her teeth sheared the flesh eagerly, she was more anxious than hungry and left the feathery bundle, instead drinking before traversing a marshy area to a line of trees by the grain terminal. The building groaned. For the cat, Lombardy poplars were poorly shaped but their height grateful. She perched. Some people stumbled by, mumbling, seeking shelter by the terminal, and later a raccoon waddled along with her kits.

The cat rearranged herself often, for the foliage was sparse. When the darkness was about to fade, down she went, and another road pulled her through a tunnel reeking of skunk and burnt rubber. Next, at the foot of a hill, barbed wire ripped one shoulder. A valley of garbage then. Up. At last the forest.

Dank, chill, coastal November. Over the duff she moved, while news of her arrival broke into twitters and rustles. Then silence swelled. Her golden blink quick as a lizard's, she focussed on finding a good tree. On a high fir branch, weary, coughing, she curled up, drew her tail over her nose, closed her eyes. Under the lids, those fluttering ducks shattered the pool again. The day went by as she rested, not soundly.

Below her sloped forty acres of woodland, bounded to the north by Burrard Inlet where headlights always rimmed the enormous bridge, and by suburban houses to the south. Logged and logged again over a century of white settlement, these acres were now home to a gas company's tank farm; to stands of Douglas fir, white pine, cottonwood, oak, Manitoba maple, and the weed trees, scrub alder and sweet balsam poplar; to brambles and creepers and berries; to a hundred species of birds plus accidentals, rarities, and visitors; to five times as many insects; and to the common urban rats, skunks, mice, moles, voles, raccoons, shrews, coyotes, squirrels, deer, cats and dogs both feral and domestic. Rarely, a cougar. To *neofelis nebulosa* most of these posed no threat, though all were unfamiliar, incomparable really—she'd known only the game ranch.

When dusk thickened, she began to travel. Simply to move meant delight, to feel rough bark give to her curved claws, to leap, to dangle by one paw, to hang by her hind legs at will, to peer through feathery conifer and shake her head against the tickling needles. Almost invisible she became, her blotches blending into the rainy evening.

Food: she smelled it everywhere.

Water: streams trickled down the hillside to the Inlet.

Shelter: trees by the hundred, though even the robust branches of the highest firs might not keep her dry. Cold was her enemy. Sunlight hadn't touched her flesh in years, but her prison had been heated. The autumn dankness, drawn into her lungs, easily followed trails scored by confinement into her bones and flesh. Stiffness came. Even though her judgment of height and distance remained superb, for thirty-six months her body hadn't lived the pounce, the snap and clinch of the canines; she hadn't rushed up a tree while her tail did its magical balancing act and the heart between her teeth quit beating.

Through the night she reconnoitred the aerial highways, thirty feet vertical, ninety horizontal, twenty vertical again. Through the trees she rippled, her sleekness attended by terror as she read the rainforest, a natural linguist. On the ground, her cold pads touched lightly as falling leaves, while vines and shrubs gave cover. Dog and cat feces lay about, near a big fence. The smell of the food those animals had eaten made her nose twitch with distaste, nor did she like that fence. Hunger insisted. Near dawn, she killed. The plump animal's blue eyes and cappuccino fur interested her not at all, but the tender fetuses tasted delicious. Then she drifted coughing through the woods towards a stream.

The cat's remains lay near the house of a social worker. This woman was on staff at a shelter for the homeless in the Downtown East Side, where each workday meant eight hours at the core of human misery and comedy.

To continue doing her job well, she travelled regularly. Among the happiest trips were those in autumn, when she and her old setter went hunting in the Interior or up north. To the faint blow of sage-brush or the rain's hum, woman and dog awoke at dawn. Perhaps the nearly winter sun had warmed the earth's surface. With pleasure, she fingered the dirt. Solitude. No voices. Once by Nimpo Lake she opened her tent-flap to meet a young coyote's serious gaze. Seconds passed before the animal withdrew into mist framing the water.

After these trips, the social worker again could look civic indifference in the eye. She could face heroin, schizophrenia, dying child-prostitutes. With skill she carved free routes around the rules. "No bullshit!" On her shifts, both staff and clients laughed, and each autumn her home freezer once more stood stocked with game. A wall displayed the deer-heads, the satin fur so dense and many-coloured, the antlers' complexity. The taxidermists, though, never got the eyes quite right, no matter whether glass or space-age plastic. She always hoped for better.

Today, her old dog's bladder and bowels awakened him before first light. Out they went, the setter's movements slow and arthritic, through her gate at the forest's edge. Gently she talked to him, rubbed his thin head for long affection's sake. He'd done his last hunt. In the year this old boy would go to his rest and a new pup would come.

He squatted. She was using her flashlight to check the state of his feces and scoop them off the damp path when he growled. Again. On his retractable leash he pulled ahead. Braked, snuffing. Where spine met shoulders, his fur stiffened. She hunkered down. Peering at the prints, she rejected her first thoughts, coyote or cougar. Smaller pads. Finer. She ran a finger around the indentations. Seeing the mangle of her neighbour's cat, she pulled that leash tight.

At home again, she clicked on the coffee maker. At the window looking north, considered. An exotic. Got away somehow. Good for you! She put a muffin in the microwave, angrily sliced an orange, fed her dog and patted him. Still uneasy, he ate.

Some damned animal mill. What do they call those killings they set up? Canned hunts. Canned!

To the east, the clamshell of the world cracked open. She sipped coffee and observed the firs' black dresses dripping with rain, the maples' last ragged leaves, the scabby cottonwoods whose bark resembled the skin of chum salmon driving upriver to spawn. Somewhere among them crouched a tropical creature.

The Animal Rescue, whatever it calls itself. They'd come. No. They'd just lock the creature into another cage to die.

She left the whining setter. Against her body the deer-rifle lay solid, its strap firm over her shoulder. The dark woods stood up like a door.

For ever after she felt that in a hunter's silence she'd walked for a long time among the trees, hearing her own pulse, but knew that only minutes passed before the cat revealed herself in the subdued radiance now flowing into the woodland from the east.

Her dapples soared to another tree. Her front claws nailed the bark as her tail curled and her hindquarters swung up to complete a perfect leap that went on, and on, as patterned brightness lasts under closed lids.

Landing, the dying animal turned her head. Pale gold eyes met the hunter, who shot her precisely between them.

Acknowledgments

My thanks to

many women friends and readers and writers, for their encouragement

John Metcalf, the short story's champion

Dan Wells, bookman, and all the Biblioasis staff

the editors of the following magazines, in which earlier versions of some stories appeared: *The New Quarterly, FoundPress.com, Grain, joyland.ca, Fiddlehead, numerocinqmagazine.com*

Dean Sinnett, whose love sustains me

The English Stories, CYNTHIA FLOOD'S acclaimed collection of linked short fictions, appeared from Biblioasis in 2009; individual stories won a *Prism International* prize plus both National and Western Magazine awards. Her earlier collections are *The Animals in their Elements* and *My Father Took a Cake to France* (the title story won the Journey Prize). Her fiction has been widely published in print and online, and has been selected four times for *Best Canadian Stories.* A novel, *Making a Stone of the Heart,* was nominated for the City of Vancouver Book Award in 2002. After decades on the city's east side, Cynthia Flood now lives in the West End on the brink of Stanley Park.